THE ONE THAT GOT AWAY

LEXIE MIERS

CASSIDY

The welcoming aroma of my favorite coffee shop enveloped me like a comfy blanket on a cold winter's night. It reminded me of the snowy evenings I'd spent sitting in front of the fire at my mother's house while indulging in a book all about love and clichéd events that were the prelude to an inevitable happily-ever-after ending.

Someone impatiently shoved me from behind, urging me forward.

"Hey! Okay, relax," I said, glancing back over my shoulder. I was stuck in a never-ending queue in a popular coffee shop right in the heart of the financial district, waiting for my morning brew. It seemed not everyone was up for being polite and civilized first thing in the morning before they'd gotten their caffeine fix. I sighed. Even though I'd been living in Denver for years now, I still wasn't used to the hustle and bustle during rush hour. People could be really shitty in the city, and I hated it.

I was born and raised in a small town called Crested Butte in Colorado, nestled between two gorgeous mountain ranges. It was an idyllic little mountain town, where everyone knew everyone, which was both a big blessing as well as an annoyance, especially for a kid. Back then, we were always safe and well taken care of, but as we grew up and became the ones being reckless... we were busted. Over and over again.

If I closed my eyes, I could still see myself riding down Alpine View Lane on my bike, the wind in my hair—without a care in the world—whizzing past all the well-maintained houses.

"Order for Cassidy!" the barista shouted.

I pushed through the crowd of people and grabbed my cappuccino, then headed out the door as quickly as I could. Luckily, I still had a few minutes to walk to my destination. Scoring an interview at one of the most prestigious companies in the city was a dream come true, and the starting salary was more than I'd ever earned in my life.

The interview was for an executive assistant's position at *Emmerdale and Quinn,* a company that specialized in insurance claims—something I didn't personally have much experience with but was willing to learn. I'd always been told I was a quick study, so thankfully didn't feel too intimidated.

The fresh autumn air was crisp as I walked and for a blessed moment, I could just breathe... until a van with a broken tailpipe spoiled the moment and polluted the area around me. I coughed and waved my hand in front of me to clear the smog.

Ugh! Gross.

At times I wished I didn't have to look for work in the city, but it's where the money was, and I needed it badly.

My little brother, Nathan—who was not quite so little anymore—had been in a terrible accident a few months back and been critically injured. He'd fractured his spine in two places and the doctors said he required three separate surgeries in quick succession. Money was tight to say the least and there were gaps in his insurance coverage. And given that he had to stay in the hospital and both our parents were gone, *I* was the one who had to work twice as hard to make sure all the bills were paid.

Of course, they weren't. I was struggling just to make ends meet. Medical bills were always insanely high, but they were especially brutal in Nathan's case. He required orthopedic surgeons, physical therapists, as well as in-patient care. I needed to go out on a limb, or we'd be drowning in debt; not only that, but if I didn't land a job soon, they'd cut his treatment due to non-payment. So, while applying for a job that required experience which I didn't have was a bold move, I had no choice. Bold was my only option, but I was surprisingly optimistic about it...

I have to be.

I crossed the street and walked along the sidewalk toward the address I had burned into my brain. To say I'd been excited to receive the call to set up the interview appointment in the first place was an understatement. Ever since I'd been laser focused on researching the company online, making sure I knew as much as possible in the hopes it would give me an advantageous edge.

I'm unashamed to admit I did do a dorky little happy dance which no one should ever be allowed to see at the time. It was the best news I'd received in a long time. I'd told Nathan about the interview when I visited him at the hospital, but he wasn't in the best of moods, so I just left him to his thoughts and got on with my day.

I was a generally positive person, but I didn't want to get my hopes up *too* high, just in case. This was a little out of my comfort zone, as well as above my qualifications, but the fact that they'd called me back to arrange an interview seemed like a good sign, or at least a good starting point.

I'd only have one chance to impress them, and that was exactly what I was going to do. I ditched my normal, casual pony-tail for an elegant bun at the nape of my neck, pulling my hair out of my face for a smarter, sleeker look. I'd chosen to wear a black pencil skirt, and short, tailored jacket paired with a light pink blouse. It was hopefully professional looking while also being warm enough for a brisk fall day.

A pair of new, but inexpensive black heels finished off my look. I hadn't paid a lot of money for them; however they were comfortable enough that I could wear them for hours and not have aching feet, which was the most important thing I imagined when it came to a job where I'd be spending a lot of my time on them.

Shit!

I grimaced. I still had a block to go, and I was fast losing time. I was going to be late for the interview! I picked up my pace and soon found myself standing before an endless flight of stairs. They lead all the way up to the building of *Emmerdale and Quinn.*

"Oh, fuck. This is going to be bad," I muttered to myself as I began to climb the stairs, one by one. My tight skirt strained uncomfortably with each step—a fashion choice I'd regret for the rest of my life. The stairs continued on like a daunting obstacle course, and when I finally reached the top, my heart was pounding like I'd run a marathon. But worst of all... a large digital clock on the glass wall revealed what I'd been dreading.

I'm late.

I rushed ahead to the mirrored glass door, and as I was about to open it, someone came through from the other side, pushing it open forcefully.

Oh no!

My coffee spilled all over my light pink shirt and I cursed under my breath at my crappy luck.

"Oh, my God. I am so sorry!" the man said to me when he came through. "Can I get you a napkin or something?"

I glanced up at him and shook my head in dismay. There was

nothing for it now. "No," I said as politely as I could in my frazzled state. "I'm running late but thank you."

The businessman walked away with an apologetic smile.

The door closed a moment later and I caught sight of my reflection. A miserable sigh escaped my throat, and my shoulders slumped. My pink shirt was stained with coffee and beyond saving. It was dripping down my skirt and onto the ground as I stood. With a frustrated sigh, I threw my now empty coffee cup into a trashcan a few feet away. I wiped my hands on the backside of my skirt.

Things can't get any worse, can they?

I took a deep breath and tried to convince myself that everything was going to be fine. Buttoning up my jacket in an attempt to hide my coffee-soaked shirt as much as possible, I pushed through the glass door. With any luck at all there would be enough time for me to visit the restroom and try to salvage my shirt and whatever dignity I had left.

The reception area of *Emmerdale and Quinn* was massive, with luxury seating in a variety of gray hues, coupled with teal throw pillows and glass accents. A massive crystal chandelier hung from the high ceiling, and the front desk was made entirely of white marble flecked with golden veins.

A gorgeous redhead wearing a headset sat behind the desk, attending to various calls like a seasoned professional. Her manners were flawless.

I quickly walked over to her and offered my best smile.

"Good morning, and welcome to *Emmerdale and Quinn*," she said with a warm smile of her how. "Can I help you, today?"

"Good morning," I said, plucking my courage. "My name is Cassidy Moore and I'm here for an interview. It's for the Executive Assistant position."

The redhead glanced briefly at the clock on the wall and her entire demeanor changed.

Heat flushed my neck and cheeks, and a new wave of anxiety blossomed in my stomach. "I'm a few minutes late, I know," I apologized. "I wasn't expecting all those stairs. I bet you're all really fit, taking all those stairs every day?" I asked, expelling a nervous laugh.

The redhead stared at me blankly, as if I was displaying the tardiest behavior she'd ever encountered.

She obviously didn't find me the least bit amusing. "Look," I said with a sigh. "I spilled my coffee on my way in and I was wondering if there was a restroom I could use—"

"Mr. Ross doesn't appreciate it when people are late. In fact, it's the one thing he doesn't tolerate," she answered curtly, with the kind of sass only a redhead could ever pull off.

I had absolutely no idea how to respond to that. I was clearly screwed if I did and screwed if I didn't. I opened my mouth to speak but didn't get very far.

The receptionist held her hand up to silence me and spoke directly into her headpiece. "Mr. Ross, your first potential candidate has arrived." She paused with a frown. "Yes, she is," she said a moment later. "I know how you feel about that, Mr. Ross. Of course." She glanced up at me with her green gaze and shook her head.

Even though my face was burning hot with embarrassment, my blood ran cold, and a feeling of impending doom slithered its way up my spine. I pursed my lips and met her gaze expectantly.

"The restrooms are up the escalator to your right, first door on the left. Your interview will be in the second office on the right. Mr. Ross is already waiting for you, so I suggest you hurry, or you'll never have to worry about walking up those steps again." Judging by the look on her face, she wasn't going to deign to give me any further advice or warnings. Her hard gaze was all I was going to get.

"Thanks," I said, crestfallen and made my way to the escalators as fast as I could. Passing through a security gate, I handed a visitor's pass to the security guard. Sucking in a deep breath, I bit the inside of my lower lip and waited for clearance.

I have to stay positive and focused.

Nathan was counting on me to pay off the mountain of medical bills we owed which were still waiting for my attention on our kitchen table.

The escalator ride allowed me to take a few more deep breaths, get my shit together, and calm down. This was going to be fine—better than fine—actually. So, what if I was starting off on the wrong foot? I was an intelligent young woman who was able to do anything I set my mind to.

I can do this.

I walked down the hallway and slipped into the restroom. Confident or not, I needed to be as quick as possible. I was already on thin ice with *Red* downstairs, and I was pretty sure she would mention her blatant disrespect for me to her boss, Mr. Ross. Hopefully, he wasn't as intimidating as he sounded.

I glanced at myself in the mirror and a whine of annoyance escaped me. Short tendrils of hair hung loosely around my face, having escaped my elegant, low bun, which was now a mess. No wonder Red had looked at me with such disapproval. I was the picture of disheveled chaos.

I had no time to attempt to fix it, so instead, I removed the hair pins holding the style in place and let my long, blonde hair tumble down my shoulders. I'd always looked better with my hair down anyway. Grabbing a few paper towels from the dispenser, I blotted at my shirt a couple times, just to get some of the coffee out so I wasn't dripping. I glanced at my watch and groaned as I tossed the wet paper towel into the wastebasket and rushed out of the restrooms, searching for the second door on the right.

Around me, people diligently worked, and it seemed a little more relaxed than the formal lobby area. The employees eyed me with curiosity as I passed, probably wondering what the hell someone like me was doing in a place like *Emmerdale and Quinn*.

I simply gave them a friendly nod. There was nothing else I could do anyway.

Reciprocation was minimal, but then again, they'd never seen me before and if I flunked the interview, they wouldn't be seeing me again anyway.

Reaching the second door, I stopped in front of it and took a deep, calming breath. then tugged on the bottom of my jacket with both hands to straighten it. Lifting my right hand, I tapped my knuckles lightly on the door and waited on tenterhooks.

"Come in," a voice said from inside. The gentleman's tone was impatient and strangely familiar. Perhaps it was true that all executives sounded alike, as they did in the movies.

My heart pounded in my chest as I opened the door and stepped inside.

The room was much brighter than I'd expected. Sunlight shined in through the large window to my right, affording a spectacular view of the city. Two teal-colored love seats faced one another, a low coffee table between them, giving me the sense that this wasn't going to be quite as formal as I'd expected. The atmosphere was comforting and serene.

The silhouette of a man dressed in a black suit was highlighted by the window. He stood with his back to me, clearly unphased by my presence.

I closed the door and cleared my throat, tucking a lock of hair behind my ear as I did my best to stand tall. "I'm sorry I'm late... you must be Mr. Ross," I said and moved toward him. "I'm—"

"Cass?"

My body froze instantly as the familiar voice echoed through my mind and my heart raced.

The man turned around to face me, and my world fell of its axis.

My eyes widened as I stood motionless, unable to move a single muscle. In front of me stood the one person I was certain I'd never see again in my entire life... or at least, I'd hoped I wouldn't. "Liam?" I breathed.

He slowly and carefully approached me as if I were a skittish deer ready to take flight.

A flood of memories came rushing back to me like an avalanche in the mountains. The football practices I watched on the bleachers in high school, the homecoming game... All the summers we spent together, the clear, starry nights, the crazy snowball fights, the hot cocoa we drank at the bonfires, and what we did on prom night. The wonderful memories of us together in Crested Butte.

Of course, another heartbeat later and the bad memories rushed back in too, drowning me like an unstoppable tidal wave. The sight of his car pulling out of my driveway; the last time I ever saw him. The tears I'd wasted on him for months after. The anguish of not receiving a single phone call from that moment. He'd disappeared without an explanation, leaving me all alone.

And they kept coming... I recalled the nights I'd spent alone, forlornly visiting all the places we used to go together. All the times I'd driven around endlessly trying to figure out what I had done wrong, why he didn't want me anymore, and why I wasn't good enough for him anymore.

Hot tears blurred my vision. Everything around me was frozen in time and I couldn't move. I couldn't break free of its hold. The memories stung just as painfully now as they did back then. I let out a slow breath... the breath I'd been holding since I saw his face. After all these years, he looked *exactly* the same, just a little more mature.

His light green eyes bore into my soul, stealing my wits from me. His familiar brown hair was styled with gel, and the traces of a five 'o clock shadow emphasized his strong jawline and high-lighted the dimple in his right cheek I'd always loved.

My gaze drank in his broad shoulders, beautiful hands, and noted how well he wore his. He even smelled the same, his cologne like a whiff of a beautiful, distant memory that was lost to the past. Everything was the same, except it wasn't. Before me stood a stranger, somebody I used to know.

2

———

LIAM

I'm never easily surprised. I've studied human behavior for almost ten years in this business. Their cues, their body language, and my perceptive nature were all partly the reason for my success in the industry. I could read people, and I could read them well, which was something not many could do. I could catch people in a lie, analyze them within a few minutes of meeting them, all the while making them feel comfortable—and that was crucial in my line of work.

As a senior executive for *Emmerdale and Quinn*, I liaised with important clients and had to build strong, working relationships with them... but it was getting to the point where I needed an assistant who could take on the tasks that I didn't have the time for. Things like coordinating meetings, sorting out paperwork, and drawing up contracts.

The last few weeks had been tough. Not only was my schedule packed with my normal responsibilities, but I now had the added burden of needing to interview potential assistants. So far, the candidates were not promising, and that didn't surprise me. Nothing did anymore. But seeing Cassidy standing in front of me surprised the hell out of me, and I was left speechless.

She was even more beautiful than I remembered. Her long blonde hair hung down over her narrow shoulders and her blue eyes were wide and bright. "What are you doing here?" I managed to ask eventually.

Her shoulders tensed at my question, and she inhaled deeply. "You're Mr. Ross."

Oh, shit... she's here for an interview!

"I am," I said with a nod. "How have you been?"

"Good."

The silence stretched between us uncomfortably. "How long have you been in Denver?" I ventured.

"You're Mr. Ross," she muttered again, the disappointment in her tone painfully obvious.

I cleared my throat. "Yes. Please, have a seat."

"Sure," she said as she took off her jacket.

I noticed the coffee stain on her light pink shirt as she sat down and grimaced for her. "Rough morning?" I asked as I joined her.

"It has been," she answered more curtly than I expected.

I shifted in my seat and cleared my throat again. "So, you're here for the executive assistant position?"

"Right, but I didn't know it was for you." That much was obvious by now. She looked like she wanted to make a run for it. Every muscle in her body was tense and her discomfort was palpable.

"If you did, would you have still applied?" I asked.

She frowned. "Getting this job isn't about you, Liam. I..."

I leaned forward. "What is it about then?"

"I don't want to talk about it," she answered and straightened her shoulders. Something was clearly bothering her.

Maybe it was me, and I didn't blame her one bit if that was

the case. After the way I'd treated her all those years ago, I was genuinely surprised she hadn't punched me in the face yet. "So, what makes you think you're qualified to be my assistant?" I asked, although I already knew the answer. I knew Cassidy like the back of my own hand, I always had, and I doubt much had changed.

"I'm a perfectionist when it comes to my work," she began. "I'm hard-working, I'm always on time, well, except for today."

"The steps got to you, didn't they?" I prompted.

Cass glanced at me and nodded slowly with a wry grimace. "Yeah. I've never been one for steps."

"I know," I whispered before clearing my throat again and glancing down at her resume. "What else do you bring to the table?"

"I have excellent telephone and computer skills. I work quickly and efficiently with minimal mistakes, and I really feel like I can be a great asset to..." her voice trailed off and her gaze met mine... "to you—to *Emmerdale and Quinn*."

I skimmed through her impressive list of scholastic accomplishments. "You attended UC Denver, with a pre-law major and a business minor, then went on to earn your paralegal certificate."

Her mouth dropped open a little and her gaze softened.

I assumed it was in surprise that I'd surmised everything so quickly.

But then she lifted her chin and plowed forward. "That's right. Business Law was my favorite subject, and I wanted to ensure I had a well-rounded education."

"You *graduated magna cum laude*, at the top of your class," I said, not surprised how well she'd done in pursuing her goals. She had been the same when I'd known her. Ambitious to a fault. She'd do anything to achieve her goals and dreams. I'd always admired her for that, and I'd loved her focus.

Loved.

"You have an impressive resume," I finished.

"Thank you. I've been looking forward to getting a job in the city that's more in my wheelhouse," she pointed out.

"Why haven't you been working as a paralegal?" I couldn't help asking. "You should be."

She shrugged, her mouth twisting in dismay. "After College I moved home to look after Mom when she got sick, then Nathan got hurt and... well, I've been working anywhere I could get a job ever since really. But ideally, I want to get back into the field that I studied for."

I tapped my fingers on the table in front of me, studying her intently for a moment. "You would be an incredible asset to this company and to me."

She stared at me quietly and pursed her lips. "Why do I get the feeling you're about to tell me that I am *not* getting this job, then?"

I shifted back on the couch. "I can't give you this job, Cassidy. Not because you don't deserve it, but because you're better than this."

"Excuse me?" she asked, her eyebrows rising up her forehead.

"You're over-qualified for an assistant's job," I said simply. "I don't want you wasting your talent here."

"Is it because we used to know each other?" she asked. "I *need* this job."

Her words stung more than I'd like to admit, but they were partially true. "No, it's not that. I don't..."

"Please tell me," She insisted.

I exhaled through my nose and decided to tell her the truth. "Look, I can't hire you because you're too attractive, you're a female, and I'm in a bit of a legal situation at the moment."

Her eyebrows narrowed. "What kind of legal situation? Are you in trouble, Liam?"

In a way.

"I'm dealing with a messy divorce. My ex-wife is relentless. She's taking me to court, seeking spousal support on false grounds." It made my whole being shudder to admit to Cassidy that there'd ever been someone else.

"On what grounds?" she asked, her tone was sharper now.

I shook my head. "She's made the allegation against me that I cheated on her during the tenure of our short-lived marriage."

"Why am I not surprised?" my high school sweetheart scoffed, crossing her arms and her legs—a *very* clear sign she was angry and upset.

I looked at her, startled. "You really think I'd do something like that? Cheat on a woman?"

"Who knows what you're capable of?" she answered snidely, obviously allowing the hurts of the past to cloud her judgement.

"Not that," I answered. "The marriage was a mistake, I'll admit that. It didn't even last a year. I was in a bad place, I was lonely..." I sighed. Surely, Cassidy didn't think I'd cheat? What sort of snake did she think I was?

"Wasn't she enough for you?" she asked, glaring as though the ten-year-old wound were still fresh for her.

"That wasn't what this is about," I answered. "We weren't a good match from the start, and I never cheated on her. She's lying to extort me for more money," I explained, not quite sure why I felt so defensive. We hadn't seen one another in more than ten years, but it still felt like I could tell her anything, even if it meant her cutting me down with her words.

The contempt was visible in her eyes now, and she shifted in her seat as if to place more distance between us.

"How do I know you're telling me the truth?"

"I am. You know I would never do something like that," I defended. "Like I said, the marriage was an error of judgement, but I never cheated her. I ended it civilly when I knew it wasn't working and wasn't what I wanted. She's just unleashing her umbrage and is coming after me for my wealth. She's aware I'm a successful businessman."

Cassidy scoffed again. "Well, I don't know you well enough to make that kind of assumption, not anymore. I just asked if you did it or not, from a legal perspective."

Her words were like knives in my chest, but once again, I deserved them. "Right. No, I didn't. Our divorce should be clean cut, but unfortunately, she'd dragging my name through the mud."

"So, you can't hire me because of the divorce, or—"

"I don't want to give my ex any more ammunition. The last thing I need is her making claims about my staff. Not to mention, we have history too, Cass."

"Please don't call me that," she said with a frown and stood up from the couch.

"I can help you get a job," I said quickly, the words tumbling from my lips and a feeling of desperation rising inside me before I could stop either. "One that is more suited to your qualifications. I have a friend who owns a law firm and you'd be a perfect fit there. They specialize in Business Law, representing companies with civil matters. They'd be happy to have someone like you there, I'm sure of it."

She glanced at me and pursed her lips. "I don't want you to do me any favors."

"It's the least I could after everything I've put you through."

Her eyes narrowed for a moment, and she took a step toward me. "I'm not necessarily ungrateful for your help, Liam, but nothing you do *now* is going to fix what you did back *then*."

My gut tightened as though she'd punched me, but I kept my composure. "I'm not that guy anymore, and if you would just give me a chance to prove that—"

"No. I can't do that," she interjected.

"Cass, please—"

"I asked you not to call me that. You waived your right to call me 'Cass' when you left me the way you did," she objected, her pained emotions evident in her clear blue eyes. Without hesitating a second longer, she whirled around, opened the door, and stormed out of the interview room.

Damn it.

I took a deep breath, my chest tight from the daggers she'd thrown my way and closed my eyes for a few seconds to gain my composure. I glanced down at her resume and reached for my phone but stopped short. I didn't want to intrude on her life... she clearly didn't want me in it anymore. Just the mere sight of me had upset her palpably, and I supposed it was only natural given how things ended between us, but her anger and pain were obviously still very raw.

I'd have thought after all this time she would have moved on and forgotten all about me, but I was obviously wrong. I sat quietly on the teal couch until Jenna, the redhead from reception, called.

"Should I send the next applicant up, Mr. Ross.?"

"No, I'm done for the day, Jenna. I have an emergency to deal with. Have them reschedule, please."

"But Mr. Ross, it's only ten o'clock—"

"Don't question me, Jenna. Now is *not* the time. Just do as I say."

"Yes, of course, Mr. Ross. My apologies."

The call ended and even though I shouldn't have directed any of my anger and disappointment at Jenna, she knew better than to question me when I gave direct instructions. With a heavy sigh, I left the interview room and rushed to my office to collect a few things before leaving the building.

Jenna was busy with a call when I walked past, but her eyes

focused on me for a moment before she cast them down to the keyboard in front of her once more.

The drive home from the office was mercifully brief and uneventful, and the weight of the world lifted from my shoulders as soon as I stepped into my home.

My safe place.

It was really the only place where I felt at ease… except for today. For the few minutes I'd spent with Cass I'd been happy again, before she'd reminded me of what a shitty asshole I was back then.

Not that I could have helped it…

A nauseating feeling rose in my stomach, and I dropped my head. I had to do something about this. Something, anything to help make any of this right for Cass. I grabbed my phone and dialed.

"Eric Hartmann," he answered.

"Hey, Eric. It's Liam."

"Liam. How are you?" he asked, his tone friendly.

"I've been better," I admitted.

"Did something happen? Has your ex—"

"No, she hasn't done anything else. This is about something else. Look, I was wondering if you still had that vacancy for a paralegal at your firm?"

"I do, but I'm not going to take on any of your girlfriends," Eric said with a laugh.

I shook my head. "No, no," I assured him. "This isn't anything like that. I was doing interviews for an assistant and this woman came in. She had such an impressive resume, completely over-qualified to be an assistant. She finished in the top three of her class at UC Denver and graduated with a perfect 4.0. She's got her paralegal certificate as well, and I thought she'd be much more suited to your offices than fetching my coffee and paperwork."

"Wow, that's quite impressive. And how do you know her?"

"We used to live in the same town when we were kids, can you believe that?" I tried to sound genuine, because I was telling *almost* the whole truth.

"Okay. You can email her resume through to me. She sounds promising."

"Thanks, Eric. I appreciate it." And I did. I'd never thought I'd be able to make up being such a shit to Cass, but I had to at least try.

"And how are you really doing? Especially with this whole... thing?"

"As I said, I've been better. I feel powerless, and..." I raked my fingers through my hair and sighed. "I honestly don't even know how I feel anymore. I just wish this would all blow over."

"So do I. You're my best friend and I know you're an upstanding guy, Liam. This is clearly a cut and dry case of a bitter ex, but you have to know this is going to get worse before it gets better. Your ex's lawyers are going to try and dig up every ounce of dirt on you they can and try to use it against you to paint a picture."

"I know."

"Is there anything that would implicate you in the past?" he asked.

I sighed and sat back on the couch, trying to think of anything remotely related to cheating or relationship issues, but the only thing I could think of was Cass. Her face flashed in my mind— that beautiful face—and her voice resonated inside me. I wasn't over her, clearly. Or not as much as I'd believed I was.

But that wasn't like this. What we had was love...

"No, not that I can think of," I answered.

"Well, if you do think of anything, you *have* to tell Morgan."

"Obviously. He's my lawyer. I tell him everything."

"Poor guy," Eric joked, which made me smile for a second.

"Anyway, I have to go. I have something I need to do," I told him, sitting upright on the couch.

"No problem, buddy. Take care."

"You, too." I placed the phone on the table in front of me and sat motionless for a few seconds before I stood again. God, I felt older than my years. Old and tired. I went and took a hot shower and changed into some comfortable clothes. It was time for a trip down memory lane.

I entered my home office and opened the corner closet. From the top shelf, I retrieved a photo album, one I hadn't looked at for months, then placed it on my desk. I sank into my leather chair and opened it to the first page. Cass's smiling face, along with me by her side, graced most of the pictures within, but as I flicked through the pages, I searched for the one photograph that I used to look at whenever I could. The one I loved the most.

It had been taken on a bright, sunny day, the last snow of the season had fallen, and Cass had insisted we build a snowman before everything turned to sludge. And of course, we did. I'd rarely said *no* to that woman when she was enthusiastic or excited about something. I'd grabbed her camera and taken a picture of her as she playfully threw a handful of snow right at me, resulting in the most beautiful photo of her I'd ever taken.

Her eyes were bright blue against the white snow behind her, and it was one of the moments where she'd been at her happiest. I'd been at my happiest, too. But that hadn't meant enough to fate at the time. We'd still ended up apart. I paged through the album, looking at her face in each photo, her expressions so full of life and love and happiness.

I'd always known when she was upset, when her brother was being a little shit, or when she was stressed out during exams. She had always been so easy to read, but I'd never realized how much I hurt her when I'd had to leave. If only she'd give me a chance to make things right between us, let me be who she deserved, but I was pretty sure that ship had sailed. *We* were such a long time ago. Neither of us were the same people anymore.

I didn't want to admit it, but those two young people in the photographs no longer existed. Our love didn't either... it was gone.

And it was all my fault.

3

CASSIDY

I walked through the revolving doors of *Sutter Rehabilitation Hospital* and smiled at the receptionist, who knew me by name now. My head was still spinning from my interview this morning. Seeing Liam had brought back so many feelings I'd thought were dead and buried.

Learning that Liam was going through a messy divorce was a bit of a shock, but it only proved to me that he hadn't changed. Whether he'd cheated or not, he was still the same selfish asshole who'd left me in Crested Butte without as much as a goodbye!

The emptiness ached inside me as I walked down the stark white hallway to Nathan's room but came to a standstill just in front of his door. I didn't want him to see me like this, all broken and upset. He didn't need a sister who couldn't keep her shit together. I had to be strong for him, and being upset over a guy from my past, over something that happened such a long time ago... was just plain stupid.

I had told myself for years that I was over him and that I deserved better. But as much as I wanted to hate him, *which I did*, a part of me still loved him. It was a part I'd tried desperately to deny and destroy, only to fail miserably. I took a deep breath, swallowed my feelings and opened the door.

My little brother was in his hospital bed, flicking angrily through the channels. As soon as he saw me, he smiled his usual crooked smile.

"Hey," I greeted him and placed my bag on the reclining chair in the corner of the room. "How are you feeling?"

"Still paralyzed from the waist down, so I'm going with not so good," Nathan grumbled. "How about you?"

"I've been better," I sighed as I sat down on the edge of the bed. "I went for an interview this morning."

"The one in the financial district?" he prompted.

"That's the one," I answered.

"And? How did it go?"

"Catastrophic," I answered honestly. "I spilled coffee all over my favorite blouse, I was late, and then when I eventually got to the interview itself, it turned out I was over-qualified according to..." My voice trailed off as Liam's face popped into my mind. His green eyes, his perfect jawline, the way he smelled like home.

"Cassie?"

I glanced up and my confused gaze met Nathan's, and I was lost for a moment.

"According to who?" he asked.

I let out a sigh and shook my head. "Oh, the guy who interviewed me. He said I was over-qualified for the job, and he didn't want me wasting my talents by being his assistant."

"Well, that was kind of nice of him," Nathan pointed out. "He obviously saw your real potential."

I shrugged my shoulders. "I guess, maybe... but I was really counting on getting that job. But now that I think about it, I wouldn't have fit in there. It was way too stuffy, and my boss would have been such a pain in the ass."

"Things happen for a reason, Sis," Nathan sighed.

I glanced at him with a frown and pursed my lips. My little brother was six years younger, but he was wise beyond his years. It was something I had always loved about him. He was the most mature male I knew. So, if Nathan was right, what was the reason behind Liam and I crossing paths once again? I shrugged my shoulders again, as it wasn't something I wanted to talk about, or even think about at the moment. I needed to spend an hour of quality time with Nathan and then concentrate on finding a job, and fast. "I guess so."

"There's even a reason why I'm in this hospital bed right now, not being able to walk."

"Nathan—"

"No, it's fine, Cassie. I'm not trying to win your sympathy or make you feel guilty or anything. I know you're doing your best, and you should be proud of yourself for having made it this far," he said to me.

I glanced at him, pursing my lips to stop the tears from spilling down my cheeks. He was the only one who'd ever called me 'Cassie'. When he was a toddler, it was easier for him to pronounce than *Cassidy* but as he grew, he'd never taken to calling me by my given name.

We spent the rest of the hour talking about the most random things, like we always did.

My visit was almost up when he said, "I found the perfect guy for you by the way."

"What?"

Impossible.

"You heard me," Nathan answered smugly.

"And where did you find this *perfect* man?" I asked, cocking my head to the side.

"He works right here at the hospital. I see him twice a week."

"Are you talking about your physical therapist, Nate?"

"So, you *have* noticed him!" Nathan winked.

Of course, I had. I noticed everything. And his PT was hot, in that young, cute sort of way which wasn't really my thing. "He's your physical therapist," I defended weakly.

"And?"

I tilted my head again. I had way more important things to focus on, like getting a job. There was no way I was fooling around with someone related to my brother's treatment, not to mention the fact my heart couldn't take another beating.

"I'll put in a good word for you tomorrow," he said with a grin.

"Please don't. The poor guy definitely doesn't need to go on a date with a woman who is neck-deep in debt. You got that?"

"You're such a buzzkill," my brother said with a dramatic sigh.

I sighed too and nodded at him. "I know, it's just who I am unfortunately." My eyes glanced briefly at the clock on the wall, and I groaned. "I'm sorry, I have to go."

"I know."

"I wish I could stay longer—"

"No, no. I don't expect you to sit here and entertain me. You have a life too."

"I do?" I chuckled and twisted my fingers in my hair. "I'll see you tomorrow, okay?"

"My PT is at three!" Nathan winked at me cheekily.

"Noted, thank you," I answered with a roll of my eyes as silence stretched between us. I slid off the bed and moved to grab my bag.

Nathan grabbed my hand, halting me. "Thank you."

"For what?" I asked, my brow furrowing.

He glanced at me solemnly. "For everything, Sis. For working so hard and taking care of me."

"You're my brother, Nathan. You're the only family I have left in the world. And if I don't do it, then who will?" I shrugged, trying hard to fight back the tears in my eyes. This whole situation made me feel so useless, so helpless. It was crap and I hated it. I crave security and stability, and for my brother to have a clean bill of health.

"I love you," he said, his voice sounding a little hoarse.

I leaned over and pulled him into a tight embrace. "I love you too, buddy." I closed my eyes against his shoulder for a moment and felt the tears make their way down my cheek. As I pulled away, I quickly wiped them away and smiled at him.

"You're crying now?" he muttered.

"I'm fine, I swear," I defended. "Being an adult isn't as fun as I thought it would be, and before you say anything about you being a burden, it's not true. You'll never be a burden to me. I'm just going through a few things, but I'm okay. I'll get it sorted. I promise."

I have to be.

"That's not what I asked, but since you brought it up, is there anything I can do?"

"You're alive, so that helps. Don't be silly, okay? You just focus on getting better, so we can get you the hell out of here, okay? Leave the adulting to me," I answered, assuring not only Nathan but myself.

"And you're sure you can manage it?"

"I'm trying," I said simply. "It's just been a hard day, that's all. But it's nothing a bubble bath and pizza can't fix, right?"

"*Right.* While I waste away on hospital food and get showers from a nurse named Fred."

I suppressed a laugh and shook my head. "Oh, my God. I'm sorry. I—"

"No, go ahead. Enjoy! Pretty soon I'll be home and annoying the living hell out of you," he promised.

"I'm counting down the days," I said and paused for a moment before turning to the door. "Bye, buddy."

He gave me a casual wave and a smile.

I took my leave, but as I approached the front desk, movement caught my eye.

Sarah, the receptionist waved me over. "Cassidy?"

"Hey, Sarah. How are you?" I asked.

"Pretty good, and yourself?"

"I've been better, thank you." I didn't know what else to say. Sarah knew my situation intimately. She'd known about it from the start, so she would understand my less than enthusiastic response. I shouldn't be so bitter, though. After all, she did care, and she'd been caring enough to help us out on more than one occasion since Nathan wound up in the hospital.

"Listen, I'm sorry, but the billings department asked me to send you down."

Of course, they did.

"It's fine," I said.

Sarah grimaced out a smile. "It will only take a minute. Would you mind popping down to see them straight away?"

I nodded. What else was I going to do? The billings department was on the same floor, at the other end of the longest corridor you'd ever seen. When I finally reached the stark white offices, I rang the little bell and was soon confronted with an older woman I'd seen on more than once occasion.

"Can I help you?" she asked, her tone formal.

"Yes, hi. My name is Cassidy Moore, I was told to come and speak to you."

The woman with spangly purple nail polish pushed her glasses up her nose and began tapping on the computer in front of her. Then she turned to me and said in a voice that made my spine shiver. "Ah, we didn't receive your last payment, Ms. Moore."

"Ah..." I echoed.

That's because I haven't made it yet.

It wasn't because I'd forgotten or didn't have the time to do it. I just didn't have the money. "I know," I sighed and lowered my voice. I didn't want everyone to know how broke I really was, and how desperate I was about to sound. "I've been struggling a bit keeping up with the bills. I'm currently in between jobs, and it's just been *hard*..."

The woman's gaze softened. "We really need a payment soon, Cassidy, otherwise we can't continue with Nathan's treatment, and he would have to be discharged as well."

My mouth fell open with shock.

No! Not his treatment! Fuck.

The woman's brown eyes filled with sympathy at my response.

"Look, if you could just give me a few more weeks," I begged, which I hated to do... but I would do anything for my brother. "Please."

The woman stared at me for a moment and tapped her fingers on the desk. I was pretty sure she could see the sheer desperation in my eyes. She sighed and glanced back at the computer, her gaze flicking over whatever information she was reading. "I'll try to postpone the date on the invoice as much as I can, but I can only give you a few weeks at best. Understood?"

I nodded gratefully. "Yes! Thank you. I know this shouldn't concern you, and that you're just doing your job. But I promise, I will pay as soon as I can. Thank you so much."

The older woman suddenly reached over and placed her hand reassuringly on mine. "You're going to be all right, Ms. Moore. Chin up."

I fought back the tears and nodded my thanks again before exiting the billings department. Taking a deep breath, I left the hospital just in time before the tears spilled down my cheeks again. I stood alone, beside my car in the parking lot and began to tremble. Then I was struck by full-on panic mode as I climbed into my car and sat there. I couldn't breathe, I couldn't think about anything, except what a failure I was. I had bills piling up and my brother was depending on me!

I can't even get a stupid assistant's job.

I lowered my face onto the steering wheel and sobbed like I hadn't done in a long time. The last time was when Liam had left me and... I growled at myself as Liam invaded my mind. Those memories still haunted me, just as much as they had ten years ago. I still clearly remembered the first morning after he left. I woke up crying—much like I was right now—because my heart hurt so much that I couldn't breathe. But I had to get up and pretend I was perfectly fine without him.

"Get the fuck out of my head!" I sobbed. I couldn't keep going like this. It was ridiculous. I caught sight of myself in the rearview mirror and came to the ultimate conclusion. I was a mess.

Again. Still. Fuck!

I wiped my face with the tissues in my car and took a few deep breaths to calm myself. I couldn't drive safely in the state I was in, so I sat for a few minutes and contemplated my horrible life. When I was finally composed, I drove home.

We owned our small house thanks to our early inheritance. We'd sold mom's family home, and the money had been just enough to allow me to buy this house and left enough aside so that most of Nathan's bills had been paid for—initially anyway. I'd moved Nathan and I into the new place as soon as I had been able to, and it had been our saving grace when money was tight. Not having to find the cash for mortgage or rent was a small mercy.

But the house was empty, and the cold feelings hit me as soon as I stepped through the door. It was empty like me. I dropped my bag on the couch and headed for my bedroom to change into something more comfortable than my coffee-stained interview outfit. After dressing in my oldest, softest sweats, I scoured the fridge for something to eat. Then I planted myself and my left-over sandwich down on the couch and covered my lower body with my fluffy purple blanket.

Ever since Nathan's accident, I couldn't sleep in my own room. The memory of that night still haunted me. Getting a phone call from the hospital to say my little brother was in emergency surgery after arriving at the hospital in critical condition after a near-fatal car accident shook me to my very core. Every time my phone rang at night, I got a nauseous feeling in the pit of my stomach before answering. And given Nathan was possibly facing two additional surgeries, I was an emotional mess.

I can't lose him too.

I devoured the sandwich in silence then turned on the television for a means of distraction. My brain was muddled, and if I could drown it out with some mindless television shows, then so be it. I heard my phone ring in my bag a moment later and I reached for it. As much as I didn't want to speak to anyone, I had to answer. It could be important. "Hello?"

"Hello, is this Cassidy Moore?"

My spine automatically straightened, and my eyes widened. "Yes, it is."

"Good afternoon, Ms. Moore. This is Lindsay from the offices of *Hartmann and Cole.* I was instructed by Mr. Hartmann to contact you with regards to the paralegal position we have available at the firm."

Holy shit!

"Paralegal position?" I stuttered, my heart hammering in my chest.

What the hell is going on?

"I don't remember sending my resume to you. Are you sure you've got the right number?" I asked.

The receptionist forged ahead unperturbed by my stuttering.

"As I mentioned, I was told to contact you, and arrange an interview with Mr. Hartmann himself at your earliest possible convenience."

Yes! Oh, my God!

"Yes, of course. When would be a good time? I'm pretty flexible at the moment." And that was the understatement of the century.

"Very well. Would tomorrow afternoon at one o'clock work for you?" she asked.

"Yes, that would be perfect," I gushed.

"Our address is two-three-five Montgomery Street. Do you require directions to our offices?"

"No, I have a pretty good idea where it is, but thank you. Do I need to bring anything with me?"

Like my blood?

I'd do anything to get a paralegal position right now.

"That won't be necessary. Mr. Hartmann already has your resume on file, and he's looking forward to meeting with you."

How that was possible, I had no idea, given that I was certain I hadn't applied for the position. "And I'm looking forward to meeting with him as well."

"Excellent, he'll certainly appreciate your optimism, Ms. Moore. We will see you tomorrow."

"Thank you so much. Have a great day!"

"You're welcome, and the same to you."

I heard the call disconnect, and my hand dropped down onto my lap, still clutching my phone. I couldn't believe it. I had an interview at a law firm as a paralegal! But I hadn't even sent them my resume, so how... Then it occurred to me, hitting me like a freight train and the thought made me shiver.

Liam said he would help find me a job more suited to my skills...

And he had. For once, Liam had come through for me. With a

heart full of hope and I tentative smile, I grabbed a nearby pillow and hugged it tightly to my chest. I really wanted to believe that Liam had changed. That he was doing this for me out of the goodness of his heart. Because, despite everything I'd gone through, a part of me still believed that deep down, he was a nice guy. He was my Liam, the one I'd loved. But my history with him made me doubt his ability to truly care, especially about me. And I certainly didn't want him to do me any favors.

I don't want to owe him anything.

But as I glanced over at my dining room table, piled high with medical bills, a wave of gratitude washed over me. Sometimes swallowing your pride was the only option.

Maybe, just maybe, things are changing for the better.

All I needed to do now was get through that interview with flying colors.

4

LIAM

"Where did you find that woman?" Eric asked when I answered my phone the next afternoon.

"Who are you talking about?" I asked, hoping he wasn't referring to my ex, as she had been tormenting me enough.

"Cassidy Moore," he clarified.

At the mention of my former girlfriend's name, my shoulders relaxed, and I sat back in my chair. "Did you interview her?"

"I did, and I must say, she is phenomenal."

"I told you," I said with a smile. If there was one thing I knew about Cass, was that she was indeed incredible, but hearing it from Eric was gratifying, especially as I'd been the one to recommend her for the position. And more than anything else, it felt good to know I wasn't delusional, my judgment clouded by the past.

"She's smart and witty, and that resume of hers is perfect. There was only one thing wrong with her, though."

"What's that?" I asked, holding my breath. Whatever it was, I was sure we could work something out.

"She wasn't already working for me!" he barked.

I rolled my eyes and shook my head and couldn't help but smile at Eric's laughter on the phone. "I'm glad you found her impressive. When does she start?"

"Tomorrow. Lindsay is drafting up her employment contract right now, seeing as I know she's a perfect fit, being that you recommended her. I trust your judgment, obviously. So, thanks, Liam. I appreciate the referral. This position had been waiting for someone as special as Cassidy, and I'm grateful you sent her my way. The business is really going to benefit from this hire."

"You don't have to thank me, Eric. I'm just glad she's a good fit."

"Oh, isn't that the truth. I asked her about the Freeding case I've been working on, in general terms, of course—just to pick her brain and observe her thought process—And she gave me a quick solution, which was *so* obvious, yet clever and insightful. I was gobsmacked it hadn't occurred to me."

I smiled proudly. "She is."

"Beautiful, too," he mentioned.

No, Eric. Don't go there. Don't make me drive to your office and beat the shit out of you!

"Look, I'm glad I could help," I said simply.

"Are you up for a drink after work?" Eric asked, his tone still jovial.

My jaw clenched and I frowned. "I actually already have plans, sorry, but maybe next time?"

"Sure, pal. Talk later."

The call disconnected and I stared blankly for a few minutes, trying to figure out my next move. A knock on my office door had me reeling back to the present moment and I glanced toward the door.

Jenna walked in carrying something in her hands.

"Hey," I said, still a little caught off guard.

"I brought your lunch, as requested," she said, placing the brown embossed box on my desk.

"Right. Thank you."

"Is everything okay?" she asked. "You seem a little more distracted than usual."

I considered my options, then forged forward. A woman's opinion couldn't hurt. "Can I ask you something?"

"Of course. You can ask me anything."

I took a deep breath and sighed.

Jenna frowned and turned to close the door behind her. "What's going on? Did your ex do something?"

"No, this isn't about her," I muttered.

"Okay. Then what is this about?" Jenna asked.

"Do you believe that things happen for a reason? That people are inserted into your life at a certain time because it's what's meant to be?"

"I guess," she shrugged.

I stared at her expectantly, hoping she would give me more than she had.

"I'm not really the whimsical type," she continued. "Sure, things happen for a reason, but I also believe that by the choices we make, we alter our path and make it how *we* want it to be."

"So, we're in complete control of our own destinies then?"

"I wouldn't use that word, but yeah, more or less. We make choices, and it takes us where we decide to go," Jenna replied.

"But what if we don't have control?" And that was how I was feeling at the moment. Completely out of control, like some god-like being was toying with me. First, bringing my crazy ex into my orbit in an attempt destroy me, then secondly, bringing the only woman I've ever loved back into my life to do who knew what...

Jenna frowned at me. "Life can't just run away with a person. You're always able to take the reins if it's taking you somewhere you don't want to go."

I didn't know what to say to that, the inner turmoil was just too real, so I gazed out in front of me in silence.

"Are you sure everything's okay?" Jenna asked again.

"Do you believe in second chances?" I asked hopefully after a time.

She scrunched up her face. "It depends on the situation, really. If a guy screwed me over, I wouldn't bother giving him a second chance."

That sounded pretty brutal. "How come?"

"Because people rarely change their ways. You know, leopards and spots and all that. We're conditioned to return to our default settings, the way we were raised."

I glanced up at her, a little surprised by how black and white Jenna was about this topic. "So, people can't change?"

"I guess they can... if they want to. But they have to *really* want to change, and I've never come across anyone who's done it successfully," Jenna said with a nonchalant shrug.

"You've obviously met some shitty people in your life."

"Yes, I have."

I gave her a half smile. "I'm sorry to hear that."

"It's not your fault," she shrugged again.

I had one more question, and considering the catastrophe that was my divorce, I wasn't sure I wanted to know the answer; but I had to ask. "Do you think I'm a good person, Jenna?"

Jenna cocked her head, and her red hair fell over her shoulder. "You seem nice enough, I guess. I don't really know you outside of work, though. But you seem to believe in people, and you give them what they're owed and that counts for something."

My eyebrows rose on my forehead, and I stared at the prickly receptionist who guarded our front desk. "That's probably the nicest thing you've ever said to me," I pointed out.

"Where's all this insecurity coming from, Mr. Ross?" she asked, stepping closer to my desk.

"I don't know. I guess, it's just everything. My ex and the case, the press... It's really getting to me. She's making me out to be this terrible person who cheated on her and has no integrity. I guess I needed someone to say they don't believe I'm the prick she'd making people believe I am."

"Well," Jenna said, "your case hasn't made the six o'clock news, so I think you're still fine. No one cares what small fish think. Those higher up know this is nothing to worry about. Your skills or reputation as a businessman have not been tarnished. Your personal life is of no concern to them, I'm sure."

"That's oddly comforting." I sighed.

"I do what I can," she shrugged with a rueful smile. "But you know, Mr. Ross, you shouldn't allow people to make you feel inadequate and unsure of who you are. You've always been a decent guy as far as I can see. You've treated people with respect and kindness, so if you need me to testify for you, be a character witness of sorts, I'd gladly do it."

"That means a lot to me, thank you Jenna."

"I mean it, Mr. Ross. You don't deserve to be dragged over the coals because she's a liar looking to ensnare a sugar daddy."

I nodded silently. It was a small comfort to have someone on my side, someone who thought I was a decent human being.

Jenna turned to the door. "I'll let you eat your lunch in peace and hold all your calls."

"Thank you. I'm sorry if I've been snappier of late."

"It's understandable. Any time, Mr. Ross," she said as she left my office.

I glanced down at my lunch, not even remotely hungry anymore. Hearing Jenna say those things to me offered a small sense of relief, but as Eric had said, things were going to get worse before they got better. And it was only a matter of time until that happened. My ex *was* a money-grabbing bitch and would stop at nothing to ruin me.

If only I hadn't been stupid. If I'd had my brain turned on, I never would have dated that woman, let alone married her!

I forced myself to eat and while I did, I contemplated calling Cass. I wanted to know how her interview went from her perspective and to congratulate her on getting the job. Despite everything that had happened in the past, I was proud of her for nailing the interview and even giving Eric a breakthrough in his case.

She was made for a career in law. She had the kind of mind that would thrive in an environment like that. She analyzed a situation from so many different angles it made my head spin, which was probably why she was still upset with me. She kept mulling things over in her mind until it drove her to distraction.

I lowered my gaze, seeing the corner of her resume peek out from under the files stacked on my desk. Considering it a sign, I reached for my phone and retrieved the sheet of paper. I dialed her number and waited while it rang, anxiously tapping my fingers on my desk.

"Hello?"

My stomach tightened at the sound of her strong, sweet voice. "Hey, it's Liam." There was a moment's pause, and I wondered for a second if she was going to hang up on me.

"Hey. Sorry, I wasn't expecting to hear from you."

"I know I shouldn't be calling you, but I just wanted to know how your interview went."

"Oh, it went great. Mr. Hartmann is a nice guy. He's so smart," she said. "But I guess you already knew that, right?"

I nodded, even though she couldn't see me. "I did. We've been friends for years."

"That's great," she said simply. "He was impressed with my resume, and he asked for my advice about a case he was handling and, in the end... I got the job. Mr. Hartmann even gave me a signing bonus, which I honestly didn't expect."

"I'm really happy for you, Cassidy," I told her. She deserved all the good fortune and happiness in the world, especially after everything she'd been through—mostly because of me.

"So am I," she agreed, and there was a pause at her end. "Listen, I appreciate what you did for me there. If it wasn't for you, then I would still be unemployed at the moment."

"You aced that interview all on your own," I answered truthfully.

"I did and I can take care of myself you know," she said, her tone laced with a slightly accusatory edge to it.

"I know that, but... we both know you needed a little boost in this instance, so a 'thank you' wouldn't go astray."

"Thank you," she responded. "I appreciate that you referred my resume."

"No, that's not what I mean," I said, bravely, or perhaps foolhardily pushing forward with my plan. Hopefully, with any luck, she wouldn't hang up on me.

"What do you want from me, Liam?" she asked, the hesitation and concern in her voice evident.

"I mean dinner, so that we can celebrate your new job."

And so that I can get to know you again, as you are now.

"I can't."

Damn it. Not what I wanted to hear.

"If it's a money thing—"

"No, it's not. It's more of an I-don't-think-it's-a-good-idea thing."

I understood that, but still didn't want to give up. Cassidy was the only woman I'd ever trusted, ever really loved. She was the one that I'd let get away, although, I'd been the one to leave. And damn it, if I hadn't regretted it every day since. "Why not? We're both adults. We can have a civilized conversation over dinner. Can't we?"

There was a long pause before she responded. "I suppose."

"Tonight, then? At seven? I'll pick you up."

"You don't know where I live," she pointed out. "But then again, you still have my resume, which was how you got my number in the first place, isn't it?"

A grin stretched across my face. "You're going to be an amazing lawyer."

"I'm not a lawyer, Liam."

"You should be."

"Pick me up at seven, my house."

I glanced at the resume and jotted down the address. "It's a date."

"It's *not*, okay?"

With a grin, I ignored that last comment. "I'll see you at seven." I disconnected the call and placed my phone on the desk in front of me, feeling giddy like a stupid teenager all over again. I hadn't been on a proper date in a while, and the nervous tension began to shiver along my skin. I turned in my chair and glanced out the window, suddenly overwhelmed by a feeling of dread.

Have I crossed a line or not? Shit. I probably have.

"It's not a date," I muttered to myself.

But it is a second chance—no matter how flimsy.

"You're going on a date?"

I whirled around in my chair and stared wide-eyed at Jenna. "When did you come in?"

"Just a second ago," she answered and cocked her head. "By the way, if you have to convince yourself that it's not a date, then it probably is."

I straightened my shoulders and adjusted my jacket, although it was perfect to start with. "It's not a date," I still defended pointlessly.

"Who's it with, then?" she asked curiously.

I narrowed my eyes at her. I didn't have to tell her anything. It was probably safer not to.

She crossed her arms over her chest. "I'm not leaving until you tell me."

I sighed, believing her. She was as fiery and stubborn as her bright red hair let on. "It's with someone I used to know... a long time ago."

"Right. So, an old girlfriend?" she asked.

I paused for a moment, then stated again, "but it's *not* a date. It's just dinner."

Jenna chuckled and shook her head. "Whatever you say, Mr. Ross," she scoffed, and turned away. When she reached the door, she glanced over her shoulder. "Wear that dark gray shirt of yours. It really brings out your eyes." Before I could say anything, Jenna winked at me and left my office without another word.

She was right—about a few things, actually. My dark gray shirt did look good on me. Gray always complimented green nicely.

But despite my foolhardy excitement, Cass had said this *wasn't* a date... so I was just going to take it casual. I didn't want to put unnecessary pressure on her or make her feel uncomfortable. That was the last thing I wanted. I just wanted to have dinner with her and celebrate her new paralegal position at Eric's firm and if fate was kind, get the chance to know her a little better.

Once I arrived home from the office, I took a quick shower. Afterwards, I wrapped a towel around my waist and stared intently at the mirror. It had been a while since I'd shaved my face completely. Usually, I only trimmed my stubble, because as soon as I shaved, I looked like a teenager again and not in a good way. It was the curse of having a baby-face. I certainly didn't want to shave and bring back all the memories from Crested Butte and hurt Cass even more, so I decided to leave it as it was.

I got dressed, opting for my dark gray shirt and paired it with a pair of tailored black trousers. I quickly styled my hair, brushed my teeth, and applied my cologne. A smile tugged at my mouth as I was reminded of prom night, when I'd spent almost an hour getting ready, an exorbitant amount of time for a guy. I'd wanted so badly to look perfect for her. My dad had anxiously fixed my tie a million times before I even left the house.

I'd felt so nervous, I'd thought I was going to be sick. It had been strange for me to feel that high-strung, as Cass and I had dated for several months already at the time, but that night was destined to be different. It had been the first night of a new stage in our lives. We'd planned on having sex for the first time, and we did, as cliché as that was.

It wasn't in a hotel room, or at an after-party at someone's house. I parked my father's truck at the end of Journey's End Road and tucked it up into the tall pines, so we had privacy. There'd been an inflatable mattress in the back, as well as pillows and blankets, and we'd spent the night under the beauty of the stars. It was incredible, and a night I'd never forgotten.

I wondered if Cass still thought about that night, whether she still dreamed about the clear sky above us, or if she had scrubbed that whole moment in time from her mind because of what I did to her just a few weeks later.

If only I could explain myself to her, tell her why I had to do it.

If only she'd listen to me! I just wished she knew the truth... that even though I'd left, it hadn't been because I'd wanted to. Leaving her was the biggest mistake of my life.

5

CASSIDY

What the hell am I doing?

Standing outside of my house, a flurry of butterflies whirled around my stomach like an anxious storm setting me on edge.

Six feet away stood Liam, wearing a dark gray shirt that made him look incredibly handsome—even more than I thought possible.

And I stood frozen on the bottom step, caught precariously between fight and flight.

Maybe he'll think I'm completely insane after this and leave me alone...

Perhaps he already thought that, but judging by the way his eyes were fixated on my body, even if that were the case, it was obvious he didn't really care.

"Hey," he said, breaking the silence.

I licked my lips, grateful for the kiss-proof lipstick I was wearing. "You're early."

"Yet... you're ready to go," he countered.

I'm nothing if not punctual—most of the time.

My mind flew back to the disaster on the stairs out the front of Emmerdale and Quinn and I sighed internally. Biting my bottom lip, I stepped down onto the sidewalk to join him. "Nice car," I said, starting our not-date off with some safe small talk. And it wasn't a lie, his luxury sedan was as sporty as it was sleek. It was the perfect compromise for a business like Liam.

Hopefully mundane chit-chat will make it less obvious just how uncomfortable I am.

I shouldn't be feeling anxious and uncomfortable, but I was. Tonight wasn't just a dinner between friends or work colleagues. Liam and I had history. A long and complex history that had ended so abruptly it still hurt when I thought about it. Yet, standing in front of him now, both of us dressed to the nines, all those bad feelings just dissipated, leaving me filled with nervous energy. It was as if we were teenagers all over again.

"Thanks, though I've been meaning to get a new one."

I scoffed at his feeble attempt at being modest but cued in on his bad sense of humor when I noticed he wore an amused expression on his face.

"I was kidding, Cassidy," he clarified. "I only just got this a few months ago."

"Right," I nodded. "Well, it really is nice. I've always liked dark gray."

He opened the car door for me like a classic gentleman. "But is it better than my dad's truck?" He grinned coyly at me, his green eyes sparkling with memory.

I climbed in and my defenses gave way. "Nothing could ever be better than that truck," I said without thinking.

Liam lingered for a few heart-racing moments before closing the door, then slowly made his way around the front of the car and slid effortlessly into the driver's seat.

I glanced at him sitting beside me, behind the wheel, and flashes of our past together appeared before my eyes. The times we'd driven in his dad's truck, singing pop music at the top of our lungs and laughing until our ribs hurt—happier times we had shared.

Our biggest argument had happened in that truck too, only a few days before he'd left. I turned away, focusing on the world beyond the window as my chest tightened. It felt like a dagger had been lodged into my ribs as the past resurfaced. There would always be the good with the bad when it came to us, and it was a bittersweet pill to swallow.

Without another word, Liam revved the engine and took off down the street.

I wasn't sure where we were going for dinner, but I didn't really mind. Knowing Liam, it would be somewhere beautiful. He'd always had a knack for finding something special, wherever he went. He even used to steal my camera when I wasn't looking and take the most gorgeous photographs. Light reflecting rainbows off the snow... a sunset where it looked as though the sun had set fire to the sky... and a simple photograph of me throwing a snowball at him looked like a genuine piece of art.

My eyes teared up, but I steadfastly refused to allow the memories to make me long for the Liam I used to know. The Liam I'd loved—the Liam who'd hurt me. Any semblance of 'us' was in the past, and even if I allowed him back in my life to some degree, he would never have my heart again. As beautiful as the memories were, I couldn't survive the pain of losing him twice.

Liam parked the car and switched off the engine, dragging me back to the present.

I glanced out the window and my brow furrowed.

Where are we?

Once I'd gotten to grips with my bearings, I realized he'd brought me to an amazing restaurant that had a fairy tale themed dining room that paid tribute to the storied romance between a winemaker's daughter and a local lumberjack—a story from before the bustling city was ever imagined—from once-upon-a-time when Denver was just a small town. It was romantic and cozy, but it also had a healthy vibe with a small live band playing on a stage. I'd always wanted to try it out for myself, but it didn't quite fit my budget with everything going on.

Once we were seated, I looked around, just drinking in the amazing décor. I was in no hurry to give Liam my undivided attention. It was strange being out and about with him after all these years. Could I bury the hatchet of the past to include him in my life? Could we be friends? I just wasn't sure I'd healed enough for that, though a part of me would always secretly want him in my life in some way. I'd likely never shake the feeling that his very presence felt like home.

"You're awfully quiet," Liam said as soon as the waiter left our table after having taken our drink order.

Not wanting to divulge the woes of my life since he left, I settled for something safe. "I just have a lot on my mind."

He nodded subtly. "So, is this weird for you?" he asked.

"Yeah, it is. Is it weird for you too?" I followed up, hoping I wasn't the only one feeling a bit like a fish out of water.

"Very," he admitted.

I sighed with a breath of relief and laughed, the mood lifting momentarily.

Liam chuckled too, but when he met my gaze, I saw vulnerability in his eyes for the first time. "I wasn't sure you'd actually agree to having dinner with me," he said cautiously.

"Neither was I, to be honest."

"Then why did you?" he asked. "After everything that's happened between us, you could have brushed me off—just taken the job and never spoken to me again..."

I hesitated and my breath hitched, not sure how much of the truth I really wanted to share.

Luckily for me, the waiter approached the table with our drinks.

I accepted the glass of red wine from him gratefully, before draining it dry. I handed it back to the astounded waiter with a sheepish grin. "I'm going to need another one of those."

The waiter hid a smile and bobbed his head. "Of course. Right away, ma'am."

Liam glanced at me across the table, his jaw dropped.

"What?" I asked. "Haven't you seen a lady drain a glass of wine in three seconds flat, before?"

The corner of his mouth curled up and he chuckled. "I can't say I have."

I tangled my fingers in front of me on the table and tapped my foot quietly under the table, full of nerves. I needed more liquid courage.

Hopefully that second glass arrives soon.

"As I said, I have a lot on my mind."

"Will you tell me about it?" Liam asked, his expression one that told me he was invested. He wanted to clear the air and open the lines of communication between us.

"Oh, trust me, you don't want to hear about my problems."

He leaned forward, his entire bearing one of intensity. "But I do, Cassidy. Come on. You can talk to me."

I *really* didn't want to get into my woes about Nathan and our finances—or lack thereof. It was a depressing topic, and even if this wasn't an official date, I didn't want to kill the mood too quickly. Despite every warning flag that waved in my mind, my heart wanted to explore whatever this was a little further before shutting it down. "First, tell me about you."

"Well, you know everything about me already," he answered. "I've been working for Emmerdale and Quinn for a few years now and then there's my fuck-up of judgement..." he trailed off, obviously alluding to his short-lived marriage. He sighed heavily.

"Up until ten years ago—or at least I thought I did," I answered with a shrug.

"How's your mom, then?" He asked.

All the breath went out of me. Liam had just unknowingly gripped the handle of the dagger I'd been worried about, the one permanently lodged in my chest, and twisted.

There was nothing for it. Unless I refused to answer him, there was only one answer to give. "She died," I said quietly, my gaze wandering across the restaurant as I avoided meeting his eye.

Liam's face dropped. "Oh my God, Cass. I'm so sorry to hear that. What happened?

He called me 'Cass', again...

I took a deep breath, licked my lips and looked him in the eye. "She was diagnosed with pancreatic cancer. It was already at stage four when it was discovered and really aggressive," I explained. "She died about nine months ago, now."

Liam's lips pursed and he took a sip of his own drink. "She didn't deserve that," he responded, his tone low and apologetic. A few moments of silence passed between us before he spoke again. "So, how did you come to be in Denver if you don't mind my asking?"

"Well, I couldn't let Nathan live in that house by himself after all that. So, I went back to get him. We sold the family home and moved out here together. I managed to buy us a small house with the inheritance, just outside of the city. Thankfully, Nathan took the move a lot better than I thought he would. He's always been strong, even when he was a kid. He's twenty-two already. Can you believe that?" I asked. It was strange how the passage of time both dragged with pain but flew by in the blink of an eye.

"And how is he?"

"He's as well as can be expected, given the circumstances," I said.

"What does that mean?"

I hated telling people this part of our story. I'd told it too many times already. But unlike everyone else, Liam knew Nathan, or at least he had when he was a kid.

"He was in an accident a few months ago and it was bad. It was touch and go at one point. He was in a critical condition. He's healing, but he's still in hospital. He fractured his spine, and he'll need to have a few more surgeries before the doctor can say for sure whether he'll ever be able to walk again. But we're optimistic, you know," I said, offering the man who stole my heart a smile. I wasn't quite sure who I was trying to reassure more—Liam, or myself.

Liam's eyes were big and round and filled with unspoken emotion.

"Cass, I had *no* idea you were going through all of this on your own. Why didn't you tell me sooner?"

I blinked, then stared at him like he'd grown a second head, and actually looked away when I answered. What was he talking about? We hadn't spoken in *ten* years. Even though we had history, why would I tell him about the very intimate and tragic details of my life during a job interview?

He's assuming a lot more familiarity here than he has any right to...

"I just did," I said. "I couldn't exactly tell you on the phone, or at my interview, could I?" I asked, one eyebrow cocked as I narrowed my gaze at him. "I haven't seen you in ten years, Liam. Ten! I wasn't going to blurt out all my problems the very first time I laid eyes on you again."

"Why not?"

I *tssk'd* at him this time and my lips pursed as if I'd sucked on a lemon.

Seriously?

"Because, knowing you, you'd want to act gallant and try to save me." And he would... he *had*. Even though he left me and never called, I knew deep down in my heart that he'd always do the right thing if faced with a problem.

"Ah."

"I appreciate what you did for me today, but I can take care of myself," I defended. "I have been."

"I don't doubt that for a second."

6

— — —

CASSIDY

The waiter returned in the middle of our discussion with my glass of wine and took our dinner orders before disappearing once more.

I picked up the glass, staring at its burgundy contents as I swished it around. "I'm not here to argue with you," I said in the punctuating silence. "I can only do and say what I feel comfortable with. You can't expect any more of me."

"No, I know. We're here celebrating the fact that you've landed yourself a killer job at a successful firm, and your future is looking a whole lot brighter now. Not to mention you have a *way* above average salary," he said with a wink.

"The fact you know all this is very unsettling," I replied, taking a sip of my wine. "It seems there's to be no separation in this. You have me at a disadvantage."

He chuckled and his green eyes sparkled brightly, drawing me in. "Eric is a friend, my best friend. You needed a job, and he needed a paralegal. The position's been open for a while, so I didn't see the harm in throwing your hat in the ring."

"And are you going to talk to him about this?" I asked and

motioned to the open space between us. "Eric my boss. Eric your best friend…"

Liam's gaze became suddenly darkened and troubled. "My personal life is personal, Cass, so no. I won't be discussing you with anyone. It's no one's business."

"Fair enough," I nodded, instantly feeling a little more relieved. The last thing I wanted was my personal matters making it into my boss's ears. I didn't just want work life, personal life separation—I needed it. "So, tell me, why'd you move here? To Denver?" I prompted, not wanting to dwell on myself a moment longer.

"To be honest, I needed a change of scenery after Duke. North Carolina was beautiful, but something was missing. My heart just wasn't there anymore," he lowered his gaze and his voice. "Maybe it was never there to begin with."

"You went to Duke, just like you wanted," I said, struggling to keep the pride out of my voice. I remembered how excited he'd been the day he'd received his acceptance letter in the mail.

Despite what happened between us, at least he achieved what he'd set out to do. I can be happy about that. How can I not?

"Yeah, but after college I decided to move back west. I wasn't sure where, but then I applied for a job here and I got it. So, I packed up all my stuff and moved. Eight years later, here we are," he said with a grimace and a shrug.

"Indeed. Here we are."

"This is seriously uncomfortable as fuck, right?"

A laugh burst from my throat, and I shook my head in dismay. "Absolutely," I said,

"Why do you think that is?" His gaze bored into my soul.

I sighed and leaned back against the chair. "You know *exactly* why, Liam. Don't play this game. We haven't talked in over ten years, like I said. The way we left things was ridiculous… and we're not the same kids we used to be."

"I beg to differ," he countered, though the truth didn't make it all the way to his eyes. He knew just as well as I did that a lot of time had passed under the bridge.

Of course, you would.

I rolled my eyes at him and took another sip of my drink, trying to make this glass last a little longer than the first one.

"You're still as beautiful as you were the first time I saw you," he said suddenly.

My heart leapt in my chest, but the reality of the situation came in and cooled my cheeks a second later. "You're not allowed to say things like that, Liam," I whispered, swallowing the lump in my throat.

"Why not? Don't you think I've been quiet for long enough?" he pressed.

Yeah, I do, but a decade is surely past the point of no return.

"You shouldn't have been quiet in the first place," I retorted. "You could have called or visited. You knew where I was. If I'd meant anything to you beyond that day..." My lower lip trembled and drank more wine to hide the emotion that would break me.

Liam fell silent. He didn't have anything to say after that, so we ate our meal in complete silence as the live music played in the background before leaving the restaurant a short while later.

A burning pain blazed in my chest as I walked to the car, stopping me from making it all the way there. I took a moment to simply stand against the bricks of one of the nearby shops, staring at the ground and catching my breath, willing my heart to be calm.

"Cass," Liam's voice broke through the pain in my heart.

I glanced up at him, feeling lost, conflicted, angry, hurt, and lovesick all at once.

"Please take a walk with me."

"Where to?" I asked, toying with the strap of my small black handbag.

"Just down the sidewalk for a bit. I think we should talk."

"Now you want to talk? We spent the last fifteen minutes in complete silence, and *now* you want to talk," I asked, unable to hide the bitterness in my tone. Crossing my arms, I focused on just taking a few more deep breaths.

"Please. The restaurant wasn't exactly private."

He was right about that. We couldn't exactly hash out the problems of the past in the middle of a packed eatery while those around us were just trying to enjoy their dinner. "Fine," I agreed and set off down the sidewalk of the hip, Baker area with him.

He led me down some steps to a small, sunken parklet that had paths lined with benches and lush trees strung with white fairy lights.

As we walked, I was grateful I wasn't wearing a tight skirt this time, because frankly, I'd had enough of stairs to last me a life-time... which reminded me of something I wanted to ask Liam. "I have a question," I said as we reached the bottom of the steps.

Liam turned to me, his eyes gleaming beneath the mood light-ing. "This should be interesting," he chuckled.

"How do you manage those steps in front of your building every day? I nearly died the first time I tried to walk them."

"I've never had to walk up those steps," he answered with a grin.

I frowned at him, demanding an explanation wordlessly. Those damn stairs had ruined my day!

"There's a side entrance to the building, accessible from inside the parking garage."

I threw my hands up in the air in frustration before folding my arms over my chest again. "Oh, my God. Why didn't anyone tell me?"

"Only staff are permitted to use that entrance, I'm afraid," he explained. "They get a special parking pass." He motioned for me to follow him.

Resigned to whatever this night was doing to bring, I did, slowly walking beside him as we made our way along the path. There were a few people in the park at this time of the evening but walking beside Liam made me feel like we were the only two people in the whole world. I knew I shouldn't be allowing myself to think such things but being with him dredged up all my old feelings for him. But somehow, for my poor wounded heart it didn't matter if he'd hurt me. If I focused on the present, the past felt so long ago.

But I know better than that.

Well, at least my head knew better than that. All the red flags of years gone by were there, yet my heart still hoped that this man I'd loved for so long would be the one for me. It hoped he'd changed, but that he was also who he'd always been… it hoped he was what I needed him to be.

"So, do you like it here in Denver?" he asked after a while.

"It's nice, I suppose. I mean, I like it well enough, but sometimes I miss the wide-open spaces and knowing everyone in town." I sighed. "To be honest, no matter how hard I try, I'm still not used to the city life. I think at heart, I'll always be a small-town girl."

Liam smiled as he thrust his hands into his trouser pockets. "That's the best kind of girl, anyway. Women in the city are ruthless and can be cruel when it comes to getting what they want. Give me a small-town girl any day."

"I don't believe they're *all* that bad," I replied, opting to avoid his gaze and his veiled words and how they pertained to *me*. "You've been here long enough. You probably have women lining up to date you," I chuckled, though it hurt me to say. But I was under no delusions. Liam was a strappingly handsome man. He looked to-die-for in a suit and had a jaw line that could slice butter. He almost certainly had women interested locally.

Liam scoffed and shook his head, and it was clear something

was weighing on his mind. "Yeah, women just love trying to take me for all I'm worth.

My chest tightened with worry.

He's referring to his messy divorce.

"Do you want to talk about it?" I asked, giving him the opportunity to spill if he felt the need. I wasn't exactly psyched at the idea of listening to him lament about his failed love life, but if he needed a friend... maybe I could be that for him.

"God, no. I don't want to burden you with my problems." He sighed. "It wasn't supposed to be like this, Cass."

My brows quirked and I gazed up at him as we continued to stroll. "What do you mean? Like what?"

"We were supposed to be celebrating your new job, but it's being screwed-up by all the shit from the past, as well as what I'm going through at the moment."

I could feel Liam's frustration, and it was authentic. "This isn't a screw-up," I consoled him, instantly wanting to make him feel better. "I'm still here, even though I'm not quite sure why," I admitted with a rueful grin.

Liam glanced down at me and stared for a while as though considering my words. We walked along the winding path in silence for a few seconds, then his hand brushed against mine.

I gave him the benefit of the doubt that it was accidental, but my body responded in a way that it hadn't to anyone in a very long time. Liam's presence, his voice, everything about him called out to me, so loudly I couldn't deny it. My head screamed at me to ignore the buried feelings, but it was hopeless. My entire body was alive with him by my side.

His hand touched mine again and this time it wasn't by accident.

I turned to look at him and my breath caught in the back of my throat.

He gazed down at me in return, his gorgeous green eyes sparkling.

Moments we'd spent together in the past flashed through my mind, making me feel more confused than ever before. Thunder rumbled in the distance and then lightning crashed across the sky, lighting up the night.

Both of us jumped.

Liam glanced up at the threatening sky with a grimace. "We've wandered a lot further than I thought. We better get going."

I jumped again as another clap of thunder boomed through the darkness, not hearing him properly. "What?"

"We have to go! There's a storm coming," he said and pointed to the sky.

"Okay!" I agreed, nodding.

We took a few steps in the direction of the car when rain began pouring from the heavens.

I let out a ridiculous squeal as we got drenched, goosebumps rising all over my skin.

With nothing else for it, we made a desperate run for it through the park.

I couldn't believe how much water had fallen in such a short amount of time. It was bordering on torrential! My long blonde hair was slicked to my head, and I was shivering cold. I had not predicted a damn rainstorm when I'd chosen my outfit for the night.

"Quick, follow me." Liam grabbed my hand like we were teenagers again and tugged me toward the closest place with shelter. It was a small, boutique hotel, still a few blocks out from the car. "Oh my God," he gushed, a smile on his lips. "That came down on us hard and heavy!"

I laughed in disbelief at our luck as I stared down at my spoiled outfit.

We were both soaked from head to toe and as I met Liam's gaze, we both began laughing like a couple of school kids. I glanced back at the park, which I could barely see through the white sheets of water falling from the sky. The rain was coming down in bucket loads and it didn't show any signs of easing up any time soon.

I turned to Liam and shrugged, hugging myself against the breeze. "It looks like we might be here a while."

"Do you want to get a room?"

I froze between one heartbeat and the next.

Is he serious? The audacity he has to think that I would get a hotel room with him!

I couldn't even believe he'd suggested it. It was absurd. It was insane. It'd be ten damn years! And yet here we were, being given a second chance. My heart galloped and the warmth between my thighs twinged with memory.

Fuck. How can I say no to this?

So, despite the misgivings of my head and all logic, I found myself nodding and agreeing with my foolish heart. "Sure." What did I have to lose?

7

LIAM

It was a longshot, of course, and part of me was joking. But when she agreed, it shocked me into another dimension. My heart pounded in my chest as I stood at the front desk, handing my credit card over to the young man on duty.

The concierge handed my card back to me and retrieved the key card from behind him. He placed it on the counter and slid it toward me. "Room seven."

"Thank you." I pocketed the card and turned to Cassidy.

She stood by the door, looking at the rain falling outside, her long blonde hair sodden.

"Cass?" I called, nervously licking my lower lip, before biting it.

She glanced over her shoulder, then turned to me. She didn't say anything, not a single word, but the atmosphere around us was electric with expectation. She followed me down the long corridor leading to the staircase, and I heard her chuckling to herself.

"Stairs, stairs, everywhere, right?" I joked.

Soaked to the bone, she offered me a grin and laughed even more, the sound like music to my ears.

We found our room quickly and as we stepped inside.

I was pleasantly surprised. The room was well lit, with a large window overlooking historic Broadway. The king bed was covered in a luxurious comforter, and plush, puffy pillows were stacked against the headboard two deep. There was a small sitting area with a loveseat and coffee table and a large flat screen television mounted against the wall. Understated elegance was clearly the theme.

"This is nice," Cass whispered as she turned to me. "Who would have known it? A little boutique like this."

I dug my hands into my pockets and glanced at her, every nerve in my body vibrating.

"What?" she asked, her brows furrowing as she eyed me.

"Do you remember the night we were caught in that snowstorm at Adam's uncle's cabin in the mountains?" I asked.

"Of course. We were there for almost *four* days. I thought we were going to die for sure," she answered, the ghost of a smile on her lips.

"That's a little dramatic," I chuckled. "Besides, I wouldn't have let that happen—not to you."

Cassidy walked around the room, glancing at the features of the suite as though she were genuinely interested in the decor, but I could feel her attention pinpointed on me, even with her back turned. "We got pretty close those four days, didn't we?" she asked softly.

"We did." The room filled with silence as our emotions palpably permeated the air around us. Neither of us had the words to break through the strained atmosphere.

It has to be me. I was the one in the wrong.

I took a deep breath. "I get that you're still mad at me for leaving all those years ago, Cass, and I don't blame you for that."

"I'm not mad, okay," she answered. "I'm hurt. There's a difference."

"That's worse," I muttered, my heart sinking. It was like she was saying she was disappointed. There was so much more pain in those words that they even stung me.

"I was hurt when you left without even telling me why, or saying goodbye," she said. "I'm still hurt. It's hard to heal without answers."

And I hated that. But how could I make her understand? It wasn't as black and white and it seemed, not on my end at least. "I never wanted to hurt you, or cause you pain, or make you cry," I said. "At the time, I thought it was the best thing to do for the us both."

She turned to me, her eyes misted with simmering hurt, accompanied by a flash of anger. "That's a lie and we both know it. Something happened that made you leave, and you were too afraid to tell me about it. You still are."

Even after all this time, she knows me too well.

"You're right. I *was* scared. I was a coward Cass, I..."

She held up her hand, not willing to give me the opportunity to explain myself. "Just stop, okay."

"No, it's true. I loved you and I left you." Why couldn't she believe the truth?

Because it's not the whole truth...

She turned on me with her lip trembling and her nostrils flaring. "That's bullshit, Liam. You wouldn't have left if you really loved me! I know it."

"I didn't have a choice, Cass!" I burst out, frustrated.

"You always have a choice. Fate doesn't just happen to you. You *chose* to leave" she spat, all her pain rising to the fore. "And don't call me that! You have no right after everything you put me through!"

I wasn't sure whether it was rage, passion, or a mix of both that caused me to storm forward, grab Cass's waist and pull her close to me. All I knew was I had to make her understand.

She angrily grabbed onto my shoulders as though she was going to shake me and tell me to fuck right off.

I froze as her fingers dug into my flesh, assuming she was going to shove me away, but she didn't.

Instead, her hands wrapped around my arms, and she kissed me, igniting my entire body.

Her lips were sweet, and the warmth of her body made me ache for all the time we spent apart—all the time we'd lost. The kiss turned savage as all the anger, hurt, and frustration of the last ten years consumed us, and became, wild, unbridled passion.

My temperature soared as my lips traveled down her neck tasting every inch of flesh I could.

Her ragged breathing caressed my ear, as her fingers raked frantically through my hair.

I walked her backward and pressed her up against the wall. Something crashed down onto the ground, but I didn't care what it was. I'd pay for it later.

Cass's warm hands dropped away as she succumbed to the moment.

My hands slid underneath her soft, wet shirt and up to cup her full breasts.

She moaned softly in my ear, arching her back toward me in need, which only made me want her more.

In one move, I slipped her sodden shirt over her head and dropped it to the floor. Her breasts looked even more tantalizing than I remembered them being. I loosened her light pink lace bra with a flick of my wrist and the material fell away to expose her perfect, supple flesh. I traced my lips along the swell of her breast, then captured her nipple with my mouth and swirled my tongue around it slowly.

"Oh my God," she moaned in my ear as her arched against the wall more deeply, thrusting her hips against my pelvis.

My erection was hot and throbbing in my trousers, twitching with need it hankered for release.

Not yet.

I teased her, kissing her now hard nipple before removing my mouth, to reach for her sleek dress pants. Slipping them from her waist, I slid them down her legs, along with her panties all the way to her ankles.

She bit her bottom lip and whimpered with desire.

My body was rearing to fuck her, but that wasn't going to happen.

Not yet anyway.

First, I wanted to explore her slowly, in a way I'd never gotten the chance to do when we were young, foolhardy teenagers. I wanted to get to know every beautiful inch of her, no matter how long it took.

But Cass obviously hadn't gotten the memo, because she began to undress me in a flurry of motion. She undid the buttons on my shirt and slid it off my shoulders.

Despite my yearning to explore her beautiful body, I didn't have the heart to interrupt her fevered efforts. So, I stood perfectly still for her with bated breath.

She ran her fingers along the skin of my torso, her blue eyes sparkling with intrigue and desire. Her fingers paused at the waistband of my pants, her chest rising and falling with anticipation.

Was she second guessing this? Was the past surging forth once more to steal this second chance? I decided I needed to take control whatever the case, and scooped her up in my arms, before laying her down on the soft bedding. Without further prelude, I crouched down at the end of the bed and opened her legs, spreading them wide and resting my hands on her thighs.

Her breathing became ragged in anticipation.

I couldn't blame her, so had mine. As I kneeled on the carpet, positioning myself between her thighs, I looked up and our gazes met. "God, you're beautiful, Cass."

A smile trembled on her sweet lips, but she didn't say anything. It was almost as if she was afraid to break the spell, to take away from the moment.

So, with no further need of words, I lowered my mouth to her pussy and tasted her for the first time. I groaned as her flavor exploded across my tongue.

Cassidy let out a soft and satisfied sigh that made my cock throb.

I'd been waiting forever to taste her, and I was not disappointed. My tongue declared an invisible vow of love to her deliciously wet pussy as I began.

She squirmed and panted toward the ceiling, her eyes closing to savor the moment. "Oh my God," she gasped, her hands grabbing at the sheets on the bed beside her.

I moved my lips away momentarily, sliding a finger into her tight pussy. I reveled in the sensation of her gripping me.

Damn, she feels incredible.

I pumped my finger in and out of her, my mouth finding her swollen clit and torturously suckling her until she begged me to stop.

"Liam... please... stop! I can't take it," she cried.

But I didn't. I wanted her to come for me. I kept sucking and teasing as her hips raised again. I forced them down, quickening the pace of my finger inside her. Finding her g-spot, I concentrated on that sacred, sensitive area until her pussy tightened around my finger.

"Oh, my God! Liam. Fuck!" she panted. Her orgasm hit her hard and fast. She arched up further, falling breathless and silent for a prolonged moment, before her pussy began to spasm and ripple, squeezing me in waves as her belly shuddered.

I silently delighted in her uncontrollable moans and gasps, then withdrew my finger to look upon her flushed and beautiful face. I wanted to give her a second to catch her breath, but the waiting was pure torture. My balls were fucking aching, my cock was rock-hard, and all I wanted to do was bury myself in the welcoming heat of Cass's stunning body.

Cass raised herself up onto her elbows and looked down at me, meeting my gaze with her own. "Please... Liam, fuck me."

I'd never imagined I'd hear those words from Cass's mouth—our first time as teens had been a very different affair—but they turned me on so much that I thought I'd explode. I stood up and watched her, as I stepped away from the bed to quickly remove my pants.

She glanced up at me, clutching the sheets, her knuckles white.

I paused, staring down at her, with a salacious and cheeky grin.

She pushed herself up on her elbows again and cocked her head, the edge of shyness in her tone. "What?" she asked quietly.

"Say it again," I murmured.

She frowned at me in confusion, her body spread out before me like a Grecian goddess of ages past.

I grinned anew. "You know *exactly* what I want to hear."

Cass pushed herself up until she was sitting on the bed, her long blonde hair falling over her shoulders and spilling onto her breasts. She pouted her lips in the most delectable way imaginable and gave me the most evilly innocent puppy-dog eyes. "Would you *please* fuck me, Liam?"

I couldn't make either of us wait any longer. I crawled onto the mattress and joined her on the bed, ready to seize this second chance once and for all.

She pulled me down on top of her and pressed her hot, naked body to mine. Her fingertips skimmed over my skin, burning a trail of desire in their path. Then she brought her leg up, resting her calf on my hip and opening her wet pussy for me.

I wasn't ignoring that invitation. Leaning forward, I lined my head up with her wetness and slid my cock inside her.

A soft gasp escaped her, and she teased her lower lip between her teeth.

I moved higher, adjusting my position until I was directly on top of her, gazing down into the crystalline blue pools of her eyes.

Cassidy rested her ankle on my shoulder in an even greater invitation.

She was wet and hot and so perfect.

How did I ever let this woman get away?

I couldn't hold back anymore. I thrust my cock deep inside her and reeled at the feeling of ecstasy that swept over me.

Cass moaned loudly, grabbing onto my shoulders and arching herself as close as she physically could.

I leaned forward with my weight, pressing my hand against the headboard of the bed, and burying my cock deeper and deeper inside, pummeling her repeatedly until I was hilt deep.

Cassidy's breathing became ragged, and she grabbed my shoulders tighter, forcing me down onto her. I thought she was going to kiss me, but instead she manhandled me, rolling us both over to climb on top of me.

"God, you're a goddess, Cass."

My high school sweetheart smiled as lowered herself down—inch-by-inch—onto my cock, undulating her hips and sending my already heightened nerves into a frenzied state of overdrive.

I grabbed her hips and held them firmly as she continued to ride me. The more she moved, the closer she pushed me to the edge of explosion, but I held on for dear life. I didn't want this to end—*ever*. I would teeter on the precipice of unparalleled pleasure for as long as humanely possible before I gave in.

Tightening my grip on her, her pussy clenched around my cock. She was *close*, I could tell. Her face was turning a deeper shade of pink, her gasps were growing louder and more ragged, and her pussy began to ripple around me. It was time to take control again. I pulled her torso down against mine and planted my feet on the bed. Then thrusting my hips upwards, I fucked her from below as fast and hard as I could.

Cassidy's fingers dug into my skin, leaving little red crescents as she groaned in my ear. "Oh, God. Yes! Harder. Faster. Please!"

Never one to deny a lady, I pounded for all I was worth, pushing her as hard and fast toward her pleasure as I could.

She began to shake, her pussy squeezing me as tight as a beartrap as another body-shuddering orgasm tore through her.

But I didn't stop fucking her. I couldn't. I was too close to stop now. I needed my own release. I wanted to fill her with my cum and mark her as my own. "Oh... fuck!" I growled. I couldn't hold back a second longer, no matter what I wanted. I thrust up into her still pulsating pussy and exploded inside her with a vengeance. An almighty groan ripped from my throat as heat coursed through my cock.

My goddess cried out above me in surprise, her eyes wide as her body milked me, squeezing every drop of cum from my body.

My shaking muscles were fast giving up on me and a cramp threatened, so I relaxed and lowered my hips down onto the bed. My arms fell to my side, replete and exhausted.

Cass collapsed on top of me, panting for breath, her blonde hair spilling over the both of us.

My cock was still nestled inside her and I didn't want her to move. But then I heard her break the moment, our tenuous, precious second chance connection disappearing.

She sighed as she pushed herself upright.

I stared up at her, just drinking in her beauty.

I'm going to treasure this moment for as long as I live.

Her hands rested on my chest and a thin sheen of perspiration covered her skin. Her lovely cheeks were flushed, and she looked slightly dazed from her orgasm.

My heart nearly burst. She was the most beautiful woman I'd ever seen. There was just no way I could hide from the truth anymore.

I'm still in love with her.

Not even ten years without her could change that. Truth be told, Cass had always been with me—in my heart.

She caught my gaze and cocked her head to the side like a curious golden-haired cat. "Everything okay down there?"

I nodded with a smile. "Everything's perfect."

A slow smile formed on her lips as she quietly nodded in agreement and dismounted to roll onto her back beside me, grabbing the sheet to cover herself.

"Oh, so now you're shy," I joked.

She gave me a half-hearted smile, the light diminishing in her eyes.

My stomach tightened. I wanted to ask her what was wrong, what was going on in that incredible mind of hers, but I didn't. Mostly because I didn't want to know the answer. Even after all this time I was afraid. So instead, I tried to cherish the silence—albeit awkward—by just being with her. I lay still, just breathing as the moments ticked on, until the atmosphere grew cold and stale.

Not even our first time in the back of my dad's truck had it been this awkward afterward. It had been awkward, don't get me wrong. Most first times are from what I've heard, but this was different... It was as if the post-orgasmic high had ended too soon and now we were left in the dark and forced to face the stark reality of the situation.

"The rain's stopped," Cassidy pointed out quietly.

I nodded. Well, that was certainly one way to break the silence, I supposed. "I should probably take you home," I said as I sat upright and slid off the bed.

"Yeah."

We dressed in silence, putting on our still-wet clothing while somehow avoiding eye contact with one another altogether.

It made me extremely uneasy.

Is she ashamed?

The ride home was just as bad. We didn't speak at all, and the tension only grew.

She spent most of the drive staring out the window, her body slightly turned away from me in the passenger seat. A subtle physical cue that she had closed herself off to me.

I was worried sick, mostly about what she was thinking. Cass had always been ruled by her head. It made her intelligent and pragmatic, but it also meant that she also liked to be in control of every situation. She wasn't normally one to take a risk, and what we had just done was a risk, and not calculated or planned in any way.

The radio played softly in the background, and as fate would have it, or whatever twisted force ruled the world, our favorite song from when we were together started to play.

I noticed her shoulders relaxing, but as soon as I opened my mouth to say something, she immediately tensed again. It was obviously better if I didn't say anything. If I did say something, I risked fucking up everything completely, and perhaps for good. Plus, it appeared she was close to tears, and I didn't want to be the one who triggered them to fall. I may not have been a part of Cass's life for ten years, but I still knew all her facial expressions, all her tells, including the one where she was about to cry.

The song ended as we pulled into Cass's street, and I stopped my car by the curb, right in front of her house. "Cass—"

"Thank you for tonight," she said somewhat stiffly as she undid her seatbelt.

"You're welcome," I said, not wanting to push the conversation past her comfort zone. Judging by the expression on her face, she was *way* beyond the limits of being comfortable.

She opened the car door and glanced back at me for a moment.

I held her gaze, and offered her a smile, not saying a word.

Then her shoulders fell, and a sigh escaped her lips as she climbed out of the car. "Goodnight, Liam," she muttered, before slamming the door harder than I expected.

Fuck.

I watched her walk up the steps in front of her house and go inside, all the while scolding myself for being such an idiot. I'd taken the wrong fucking course of action! I'd let fear and worry guide me instead of trusting my deepest gut instincts and my heart.

I should have said something, anything!

As I drove away, sadness dragged at my spirit. So much for second chances. Maybe this was the way it was always supposed to go? Perhaps my beautiful Cass was destined to remain the one that got away...

8

CASSIDY

A couple days after my roll-in-the-hay with Liam, my first day at my new job arrived! I blinked open my eyes and a beam of sunlight flashed directly onto my face, blurring my already hazy vision and making me curse under my breath. With a groan, I rolled over. I stared at the clock beside me on the wall and sighed. It was two minutes before my alarm was supposed to go off and I had a chink in my neck from another night spent on the couch. "Damn it."

I sat up and images of my time with Liam flooded back into my mind, followed by a sweeping wave of sadness. The night I'd spent with Liam had been one of the greatest nights of my life, but also one of the worst. And more importantly, it had been a mistake.

A huge mistake.

Tt had been amazing and spontaneous, but if it wasn't for Liam being... Liam, I could have gone my whole life without a memory like it. I'd just set myself up for more heartbreak.

Since when do second chances work out, anyway? I mean, if we didn't work out the first time, why would now be any different?

71

I sighed and snuggled back down beneath the warmth of my covers on the soft, suede couch. I still couldn't believe that Liam had *nothing* to say to me in the car while our favorite song had played on the radio, or even when he'd dropped me off. He'd offered no words, no explanation, nothing.

As usual.

And for two days following, he hadn't bothered to call me. He hadn't even texted! It's almost as if he were treating me like a flashback booty call... and I fucking hated it. That wasn't me, not by a long shot. But I only had myself to blame if I'd thought he could really change. His M.O was disappearing without an explanation and that clearly hadn't changed.

Stifling a yawn, I glanced at the outfit I'd draped over a nearby chair. It was time. I couldn't put the day off anymore. It was going to start without me if I didn't get a wriggle on. "Okay... get up, Cass," I encouraged myself.

Climbing out of bed, I made myself a cup of coffee and glanced at my phone with pursed lips. There were no messages or calls from Liam. *Still.* Disappointment hit me like a punch to the gut and I groaned aloud. I'd thought maybe—just maybe—he'd text or call to wish me good luck at my new job. But again, I'd made the mistake of allowing myself to be disappointed. "Ugh. Come on, Cass! Get it together."

Maybe he'll call later today? Maybe he just doesn't want to throw me off my game... Isn't there some kind of rule where guys have to wait three days before calling, anyway?

I shook myself to clear my thoughts. Regardless of what my vagrant high school sweetheart chose to do, I had bigger fish to fry today.

Today being my first official day at *Hartmann and Cole*, I was determined to have a great day and make an even greater impression. I also had to find the time to swing by the hospital to make another payment toward Nathan's treatment. Mr. Hartmann's signing bonus was more than generous and would easily cover the next few months.

I'd almost burst into tears when he'd offered me the bonus. It had seemed too good to be true on top of landing a secure, high paying job. And even better than that, after having signed the contract just three days ago, the balance had already been deposited into my bank account. I was beyond grateful and had absolutely no words to properly express it, so I figured the best way to show my true gratitude would be to show up and work hard.

Within the hour I was dressed in a chic outfit, my hair swept to the side, ready to go. And despite everything that had happened over the last two days, I was feeling quietly confident. I drove to the hospital and walked along the corridor, my heels clicking along the polished concrete floor until I found the billings office.

"Good morning, ma'am. May I help you?" the young woman greeted me with a warm smile.

"Morning," I greeted in return and pulled out my wallet. "I'm here to make a payment on the account of Nathan Moore. I'm his sister and responsible for the account."

"Of course," she answered and typed away on her keyboard as she looked up the details of the account. A moment later she took my card from me and swiped it through the machine. "There you go."

The relief in my heart at knowing I could pay this bill was overwhelming. It felt like a mountain had been lifted from my shoulders, at least for the moment. This downpayment would give me time to breathe. "Thank you," I said, accepting my card back, before leaving with a smile. With a bounce in my step, I made my way to Nathan's room. When I opened the door, I found the doctor standing beside Nathan's bed.

"Hey, Cassie," Nathan said with a welcoming smile. "You look nice, today."

I winked at him and approached the doctor to find out if there was any news I should be aware of. "Good morning, Dr. Andrews."

"Good morning, Cassidy."

"How is everything going?" I asked, looking at my brother.

"Look at this!" Nathan said excitedly and pointed to his feet.

As soon as I saw him wiggling his toes, I stopped breathing and bit my bottom lip.

This is too good to be true!

"Oh, my God. Nathan! You can feel your toes?"

"Yep! It's pretty impressive, right?" He grinned proudly.

"Doctor, is this normal?" I gasped, sucking in a deep breath. "I mean, I'm not ungrateful. I just didn't expect him to make so much progress this soon. A part of me was afraid he may never walk again," I admitted.

"Nathan is a very strong-willed young man," the doctor answered as though that was the entire medical answer to this very unexpected development.

I couldn't help laughing. "Don't I know it."

"Usually, with injuries as extensive as Nathan's, the prognosis is not very good, but despite that he's exceeded our wildest expectations. And with the way things are currently progressing, coupled with his impressive determination, there may not be a need for another surgery. With willpower, physical therapy, and time... we might find him back on his feet before we ever imagined it."

My eyebrows shot up. With news like that I could breathe again. I glanced at Nathan, who was still proudly wiggling his toes. A relieved tear ran down my cheek, but I quickly wiped it away. I didn't want to ruin my makeup before I even got to work. "That's the best news I've heard all month."

"Apart from getting a job at a fancy law firm, Sis," Nathan pointed out.

Dr. Andrews glanced at me and smiled. "Congratulations, Cassidy."

"Thanks," I said, offering an enthusiastic smile. "Speaking of which... I have to get going, I'm sorry, or I'll be late my very first day."

"We wouldn't want that," Nathan said.

"Thanks for stopping by, Cassidy," Dr. Andrews said.

"No, thank *you* for giving us such great news!"

The doctor glanced at my brother. "It's Nathan you must thank. He's the real champion here."

"He is, isn't he?" I agreed as I glanced at my little brother, struggling against the tears that threatened to spill once again.

He was twenty-two years old, but he'd always been far wiser than his peers. Nathan was the one who'd helped me move on with my life after Liam. So, he likely wouldn't be too impressed with me if he knew what Liam and I had gotten up to a few nights ago.

My skin still tingled with a ghostly memory of where Liam had touched me, and oddly, despite all my head's protestations, I had to stop myself from grinning like a lovesick teenager whenever I thought about it. No, I couldn't let my brother know about our hook up. He'd be furious and rightly so.

Nathan knew how much Liam's departure had affected me. He'd heard me crying in my room for more nights than I dared to count. He knew how long it had taken me to recover from that loss and get over everything that had happened—which was why I knew he'd want me to stay as far away from Liam Ross as humanly possible.

But I can't.

"Cassie?" Nathan's voice snapped me back to the present.

Back to his hospital room, with Dr. Andrews staring at me strangely, his head cocked to the side as if observing me.

"Oh, sorry!" I apologized. "I think I zoned out there for a minute. I'll be back later to tell you all about my day, okay?"

"Okay, sounds good. Could you maybe bring me back some pizza or Thai food?" Nathan asked.

I glanced at Dr. Andrews, who held his hands up in defeat. "It's fine by me. This kind of willpower certainly deserves to be rewarded."

"Great!" Nathan smiled happily and glanced expectantly at me.

If my miracle brother wanted pizza, he could damn well have pizza! "Whatever you want, little brother," I said to him. "I'll see you later."

I left the hospital feeling lighter than I had in a *very* long time. Nathan's bills were current, he was getting better, and from the sounds of it most probably wouldn't require any further surgery! And on top of that, I had an amazing new job with an incredible salary. Everything was finally falling into place.

The only piece of my new life's puzzle that I wasn't so sure about was Liam.

Where does he fit in?

We'd had sex—very passionate sex, I might add—but where did that leave us, exactly? The better question was, did I have the fortitude to allow him back into my life after everything that had happened? Was our one night of frenzied passion all it took for me to go back on all the promises I'd made myself?

What if he leaves me again?

I'd barely survived the first time, so I was sure as hell I wouldn't survive it a second time. Did he even want to be a part of my life again? I had so many questions and not nearly enough answers! Somehow, Liam had weaseled his way back into my life, and into my pants as well.

As I climbed into my car and put my seat belt on, my breath caught in my throat. I could still *feel* the pressure of his hands against my breasts as he thrust himself inside me, over and over.

Damn, that was hot...

Shivers ran down my spine and I glanced at myself in the mirror with a look of disapproval. "No, Cassidy. Stop it." I had to focus. I couldn't be thinking about fucking my Ex on my first day of work. Especially not Liam. It was his best friend's firm. That would be unprofessional, not to mention totally inappropriate.

Not that anyone would know...

I sighed as I started the car. This was already getting too complicated. The drive from the hospital to the office was brief, and I kept the window open for some fresh air to clear my head.

At my new work, everyone was surprisingly friendly and helpful as I found my feet. Mr. Hartmann... or *Eric,* as I was told call him, was nice, and he briefed me about many of their most important cases. It was a lot to remember but I didn't mind. The high stress, busy environment was exactly what I had always desired. I loved it already.

At lunchtime, I took out my phone and texted Liam, even though I *knew* I shouldn't. But I couldn't help it. I wanted to meet up with him. I needed to talk about the other night and what it meant for us—what it meant to him. I used to understand Liam so well when we were younger. I knew how to read his physical cues, his eyes... and all the subtle hints on his face that most people missed. Now, I was a little out of sorts. So much time had passed... I didn't know what to expect, or what he was thinking anymore.

"Boyfriend trouble, Cassidy?" Hannah, one of the paralegals, asked me as she sat down next to me.

I glanced up from my phone and pursed my lips. "No, I was just texting a friend." It wasn't a lie... we weren't back together yet.

"You were pretty zoned out while typing that message," she pointed out.

"It's nothing," I shrugged, not wanting to explain my whole life story to someone who was practically a stranger.

"How's your day been so far? Not too much for you to handle?" Lennox, one of the managing partner's paralegals, asked.

"No, quite the opposite. It's exactly what I hoped it would be. My previous job was much less stimulating, and I was bored out of my mind. Plus, I loved Business Law in college, so this is right up my alley."

"Eric said you were a UC Denver girl, top of your class. That's impressive," Hannah offered.

I glanced at Hannah, who was the same age as me, but so different in her appearance. She had glossy black hair, olive skin, and high cheekbones. Her big, brown eyes and pink lips reminded me of my old Columbian roommate. I'd always envied her beautiful skin and features, and the way she'd had the college guys hanging on her every word.

Hannah was also one of those girls, I could see it as clearly as day. And the worst part was, I was totally jealous of her as well. But there was one thing no one could take away from me, and that was that I graduated at the top of my class. "Thank you."

"Why didn't you just become a lawyer?" Lennox asked and glanced at me after taking a bite of her sandwich.

"Yeah, what kept you from law school?" Hannah chimed in.

I pursed my lips and lowered my gaze. "I was going to go, but..." I took a deep breath and ran my fingers through my hair. "My mom got sick, and I had to go back home."

An awkward silence filled the air. "I'm so sorry," Hannah said.

"It's okay. You didn't know." I glanced at everyone around the table. "None of you did, so stop it. It's okay, really."

"So, is your mom okay now?" Keith, another paralegal at the firm asked.

"Keith," Hannah muttered under her breath, giving him the side-eye.

"Sorry," Keith mumbled.

I cleared my throat and stood up. "I just need to make a quick call. Excuse me." There was no better time to call your ex-boyfriend whom you'd recently slept with, than when you're already drowning in self-pity... I dialed Liam's number and waited for him to answer.

"Hey, it's Liam Ross. I'm not available right now. Please leave a message and I'll get back to you as soon as I can. Alternatively, call the office if it's urgent."

After the beep, I left a message. "Hey, Liam, it's Cassidy. I was just hoping you'd have replied to my text, but I guess you're busy with work. I'd really like to get together after work tonight, if you can? Call me back, please. It's important." I ended the call and took a few deep breaths.

My ridiculous imagination was off to the races, running wild and drawing conclusions of its own—all because he hadn't texted me back. With a concerted effort I tried to find my calm.

There were a hundred possible reasons as to why he wasn't answering his phone, and considering we'd only slept together *once since* becoming reacquainted, I really needed to chill. How did this guy still manage to consume me after all these years? He was like a drug. A heart-achingly handsome blast from the past that had me hook, line, and sinker. It'd been *so* long since I felt good—since I'd been happy—it was an addictive feeling and hard not to chase.

Not wanting to seem desperate and reveal the extent of my feelings, I focused on my next task and pushed Liam to the back of my mind. I was a pro at doing that, I'd been doing it for over a decade now.

What's one more day?

I went about my day and even managed to leave my phone in my bag in the staffroom, so that I couldn't keep checking it. If he called, he could leave a message, just like I had with him. The day passed quicker than I thought it would, and I was even complimented by Eric who was thoroughly impressed with my work, which meant a lot to me.

After work, I picked up some pizza for Nathan, and headed over to the hospital. I glanced at my phone every so often on the drive over, but there was still nothing. No phone call, no text, and no messages from Liam.

It was after six when I finally stepped into Nathan's room and my baby brother was looking very cheerful. I put on my brave face and told him all about my day. How much fun I'd had... how nice the people had been... and how much I'd already learned.

Nathan was happy for me, and we spent a good two hours together.

Of course, I didn't mention Liam. But I didn't know how long I could keep the truth from him, I *really* didn't like keeping things from my brother, period. He was the only family I had left. And as his big sister, it was my duty to put my personal problems aside and stay upbeat and positive for him. His recovery was paramount, after all.

I'll deal with Liam later.

9

———

LIAM

Two calls and four texts—all without a single reply from me. That was what I had to deal with when I glanced at my phone the moment I stepped out of the courthouse. As if I didn't have enough to deal with today. It had been a *long* day, and I was exhausted. Seeing my ex-wife and her smug-as-shit lawyer from across the courtroom made my insides churn with palpable rage; rage at her and at myself. Marrying that woman was the biggest fuck-up of my adult life.

By the end of the day, I was wondering why I'd want anything to do with a woman ever again. So, seeing all of Cass's texts and messages made me uneasy to say the least. I didn't want everything with her to blow up in my face too. That was the last fucking thing I needed.

"Liam!" Morgan called my name. and

I lowered my phone and looked up. Morgan's straight posture spoke of a confidence I lacked now.

My Ex's lawyer had been ruthless in his statement about our martial life and even though I was told not to say a single word to him during the hearing, it had been extremely hard to keep quiet against all the slander he unloaded at my expense.

"Are you okay?" Morgan asked. "It was pretty brutal in there."

"Yeah, I'm fine," I lied.

Morgan Cole had been my lawyer for a long time. I trusted him with all of my legal concerns. We were initially introduced by Eric, as Morgan and Eric were partners in their law firm. Eric suggested I hire Morgan to represent me, and I understood why. Eric and I were friends, and we didn't want a conflict of interest on our hands by crossing the lines of our personal lives with our business lives.

But Morgan was a great attorney, and although I was taking a battering now, I had hope that I would come out on top, with my integrity and reputation intact. I was just bloody tired and over the day in general.

"Listen, Liam. I know you're frustrated right now, and I can understand that, but the trial may go on for three days, yet so you've got to hold out for a little longer."

"I know." I sighed.

"And you can't see *her*" he said discretely, referring to Cassidy, "until all of this is over. You know that too, right?" Morgan warned.

"Yeah, I know."

Even if it means losing the only woman I've ever wanted.

"If your Ex's lawyer finds out about this—"

"I know!" I snapped, my temper fraying.

What the fuck else does he want from me? A pint of blood?

I glanced back at my phone and tried again to calm down. I'd told Morgan about what happened with Cassidy, obviously not in too much detail, but I felt like I had to tell him. I didn't want him to be ambushed by any surprises from the opposite counsel because I'd withheld information. He needed to know everything, including who I was sleeping with... which was why he'd advised me to stay away from Cass until everything blew over.

It's for her own safety and mine.

But why was it hell of a lot harder than I thought it was going to be? My Ex's lawyer didn't need any more ammunition against me than he already *allegedly* had. Not only was my reputation on the line, but my credibility and my career as well. Losing a case where my integrity had been brought into question would not do me any favors, especially with the company I worked for.

I could lose my job if the judge found in my ex-wife's favor. Word travelled fast in the upper echelons of society. But maybe my receptionist was right. Maybe it would be okay...

I'd spent the last few months thinking over every little detail of the case. I tried to think back on all the time I'd spent with my Ex... all our interactions over the past eighteen months, trying to figure out if there was something, *anything*, that I'd done that would make me look guilty of infidelity. But there was nothing, no other woman, no late-night calls to female friends—nothing! She was grasping at straws.

Surely, the court will see that?

I knew guys that took advantage of women, real bad guys. Men that cheated, lied, used, and abused. But that just wasn't me. You could accuse me of being a workaholic, of being lazy around the house, and being emotionally cold when it came to business.

But not this.

I respected women, whether they were related, friends, work colleagues, or acquaintances.

But my words aren't enough.

It didn't matter that I was a respected expert in my field, who'd never taken a wrong step. When the shit hit the fan, people tended to forget about all the good things you'd done in your life and instead focused on rumors and gossip. No matter how much it cost or how long we had to fight it, I wasn't going to let her win.

I couldn't. Not only would it be an injustice, but I'd end up shelling out marital alimony for the rest of my damn life and there was *no way* I could accept that.

This wasn't a loyal, loving wife I'd had for years, and we'd decided to go our separate ways. This was a woman who'd taken me for a ride, bled me for every cent she could, exploiting me to live the good life, only to make up vicious untruths about me in the end. I wasn't going into a lifetime of debt for a fuck up that had amounted to less than eighteen months of relationship!

That's fucking bullshit.

I understood why Morgan had advised me to keep my distance from Cass. After all, she was an employee at Morgan and Eric's firm—the firm that represented me. It was more than a personal conflict of interest, it brought business into it and just as I had hired Morgan over Eric, I had to keep the paths from crossing to keep everything above board and safe for everyone involved.

Hadn't thought that one through when I'd recommend her for the job.

Not only that, but I also didn't want my Ex's lawyer to see us together and find out that we were... My thoughts stopped abruptly.

What are we, exactly?

We'd slept together a couple of nights ago and gone to dinner, but that was really all there was. And as much as I wanted to think that we had a future together, I also had to accept that it might never happen. There were just too many variables, the heaviest of which was a decade of time spent apart. It had been a spur-of-the-moment transgression of passion for us both. And it had left us with more unexplained feelings and unanswered questions than we'd started with, all of which could not be ignored if there was any hope of us reconciling.

Maybe I should explain to her that we just need to put our relationship on hold for a while?

But there were issues with that approach. She'd think I only wanted to be with her on *my* terms, and that wasn't going to sit well with her; especially as I was the asshole that had left her high and dry in the first place. I certainly couldn't afford to hurt her again, but I also couldn't provide her with a future if I didn't *have* one to offer. There was simply nothing else I could do. Not until the trial was over.

Leaving Morgan with my apologies for being so short with him, I went home, exhausted and frustrated. My phone buzzed a few times, and I groaned aloud. It was probably Cass, and I just didn't have the mental bandwidth or strength to talk to her. I ran my hands over my face as I collapsed into my recliner. I wanted to talk to her, God knew I did, but *I* knew that I'd be curt with her, and she didn't deserve that after everything I'd already put her through.

Relaxing into my recliner, I thanked the universe that my house was dark and quiet, as it always was. I dropped my keys down on the lamp table beside me, along with my phone and wallet.

I need to get out of these clothes. Damn it.

With another groan, I forced my tired body to stand once more and walked to my bedroom. I slipped off my jacket and my tie, draping them over the backrest of the couch as I moved past. Running my fingers through my hair, I let out a miserable sigh as my phone buzzed again.

She isn't going to let up, is she?

Guilt tightened my gut. But instead of answering, I ignored the messages and took a relaxing hot shower. I closed my eyes beneath the steaming water and hoped my troubles would wash down the drain.

If only it were that simple.

When I climbed out of the shower, I slid on a pair of comfortable track pants and a t-shirt before I reheated some leftovers that were in the fridge and grabbed a beer. Fuck knew I deserved it. Actually, I deserved a whole bloody liquor store's worth of liquid relaxation if were being honest. I sat down on the recliner again and ate my dinner, catching up on the sports news of the day. I'd always been a fan of basketball and football, ever since I was a kid. I'd always watched it with my dad. Most of our father-son bonding times had happened on our old black couch in the living room of the house I grew up in, back in Crested Butte. I missed my old man.

Maybe I should call him?

I needed a bit of guidance and fatherly advice, that was for sure. Finishing my beer and dinner, I grabbed my phone and dialed my father's number.

"Hey, Son," my dad's voice sounded over the line.

"Hey, Dad. How're things going?"

"Good, buddy. Your mom's planning a trip down to Denver at Christmas if that's okay?" my dad said.

"Of course, Dad. That'd be nice. It feels like forever since you guys came to visit."

"It's not like we get invited, or anything," my father joked.

"You know you and Mom are always welcome," I countered.

My father scoffed. "Oh, we wouldn't want to impose on your big city life."

I rolled my eyes up to the ceiling and ran a hand through my hair. "It's not as glamorous as you might think. I'd much rather be sitting on that black couch in your living room, drinking beer and watching football."

"Is everything okay?" my father asked. "You sound... off."

I rubbed my eyes with my free hand. "There's been a lot of things happening lately."

"Besides the divorce lawsuit?" he asked.

My stomach tightened. I *hated* that my parents had to deal with the lie that I was some sort of cheating bastard. That was *not* the reputation I'd had back home.

"Yeah."

"Do you want to talk about it?"

Yep. I do.

"I saw Cassidy a few days ago," I said, swallowing the uncomfortable lump in my throat.

"Cassidy Moore?" The surprise in my father's voice was clear as day.

"Yes, that's her." For some reason I'd thought my dad would forget who Cass was, but then again, she was kind of *unforgettable.*

"You haven't spoken about her in a while. How is she?"

"She's great. She just got a job at Eric's firm as a paralegal. She's just as beautiful as the last time I saw her."

"And? How'd it go, seeing her again?"

I shifted in my seat and shrugged my shoulders, even though my dad couldn't see me. My dad knew the complicated history between Cass and I, as well as the circumstances around how everything had ended. He also knew just how much it had broken me to leave her.

"It was... strange. We talked, we went out to dinner downtown, then we took a walk. Everything felt exactly like it used to. It started to rain so we ran for cover and ended up at a small hotel."

"Liam—" By the tone of my father's voice, he already knew *exactly* what had happened.

"I know what you're thinking, Dad. It was most probably a mistake, a big one, but everything I felt for Cass is still there and seeing her again just made it come back even stronger."

"So, what are you going to do about it?"

My father's question took me by surprise, and I inhaled

slowly, because I didn't know the answer. "Right now... I can't do anything about it. Morgan told me to keep my distance from her until the lawsuit's settled. I don't want people to think I'm a bigger scumbag than they already believe I am."

My father scoffed and cleared his throat. "Does Cassidy know that you're doing this?"

"Dad, I can't just tell her that—"

He cut me off. "Liam, she deserves to know the truth, or she'll think of something even worse in the silence, trust me."

I groaned and put my head back against the head rest and looked up at the ceiling. "She's going to think that I'm full of shit, Dad."

"And if you explain it to her, then you are," my father pointed out.

I could see him sitting at the kitchen table, a cup of black coffee in his hand, dishing out wisdom the way only he could. He was one of the wisest people I knew, and not because he was my father. Even though he'd never tell me outright to do something, he'd always gently guide me into finding the right path myself. Clearing my throat, I gathered the courage to admit what I was really worried about. "Either way, I'm screwed."

"Do you love her?"

I froze. Did I? A lot of time had passed between us, but... "Yeah, I do."

"And does she know that?"

I paused for a moment too long. I'd always thought she knew how I felt, but from her reactions yesterday, I had to acknowledge that was not the case.

"You should tell her, Liam. And if she still loves you, it won't matter that you're going through a tough time, dealing with a messy divorce, or anything of the sort. That's the best thing about love. It's not conditional of circumstances. She'll understand, Son. She'll come around. You just have to communicate and be honest.

Giving her radio silence won't protect her. It'll just hurt her more and I know you don't want that."

I closed my eyes and nodded. He knew me too well. "Thanks, Dad."

"You're welcome, buddy."

"Tell Mom I send my love, okay?"

"Of course. She's at Rhonda's, next door. I'll give her the message."

"Thanks, Dad. I can't wait to see you guys. I really miss you."

"We miss you too, Son. Keep your chin up, okay?"

"I'll try my best, Dad. Bye." I lowered the phone as soon as I heard the call disconnect and a wave of nostalgia crashed over me. I really missed my parents. They were only a few hundred miles away, but it sucked that I couldn't see them as often as I would like because I was always so busy with work. I hated to think of them all alone in their house in Crested Butte, the same house I grew up in, the same house Cass and I spent many afternoons and nights in.

At times I wondered what my life would have been like if I had stayed there. Would Cass and I have gotten married and had a little family? Would we have grown old there, or would we have settled somewhere else? Or would we have split anyway, given our dreams were so different?

A sudden banging on my front door startled me back to reality. I jumped up from the couch and walked to the front door. I opened it slowly, not sure what to expect on the other side. "Cass?" I said, shocked. "How'd you find me?"

"You're listed!" she spat as she stood in front of me, her blue eyes wild and angry.

I immediately stepped to the side, an unspoken invitation for her to enter.

Indignant with emotion, she just stood there, her breathing erratic.

"Do you want to come in?" I prompted.

She pushed past me and stormed inside, her eyes already glazed with the onset of tears.

I closed the door.

Shit. This is going to be interesting.

I followed her to the living room and waited for her to speak. She obviously had a heart full of hurt to unload and I wasn't going to force her to talk until she was ready.

She whirled around, her expression pained. "What the hell is going on with you, Liam?"

"What do you mean?" I asked.

"You know *exactly* what I mean, you asshole! You practically begged me to give you a second chance... and stupidly I did! We had a great night, you fuck me at the hotel, you ghost me for three days, then ignore my calls and messages all day. Do you know how fucked up that is?"

"Wait, Cass," I said, holding my hands up in defense. "If you let me explain—"

"Was the other night a mistake?" she exclaimed, a tear streaking down her lovely, flushed cheek.

"It's not like that," I muttered as I stepped away from her.

"Then what *is* it like, Liam?" she asked,

Even though I knew it was imperative to speak, I still couldn't bear to meet her gaze.

"I spent the entire day trying to call you. I even messaged you that I wanted to talk and said it was urgent, yet you still ignored me."

"Cass—"

"Do I mean so little to you that you think you can just use me like that? Like some damn city booty call? Did you want a taste of the of the smalltown life again?"

Don't put it like that.

"Cass, I didn't use you."

"It sure as hell feels like it. If it was such a big mistake, why didn't you just say so? Why didn't you put a stop to things before they went as far as they did?" she asked, hastily wiping her tears away with her sleeve.

The room fell quiet, and I slowly turned to her. "You mean a lot more to me than you think you do, Cass. I just wish I could make you see."

The fight seemed to go out of her like a deflating balloon as her shoulders slumped. "Then why the silence?" she pleaded. "I had to lie to my brother as to why I was constantly checking my phone. You know I don't like lying to my brother, Liam. He's all I have left."

"I know."

"Then what the fuck?" she repeated in frustration, throwing her hands up in the air, before pressing her palm to her face.

"I thought about you every single moment of every day." It was the truth.

Cass raised an apprehensive eyebrow at me and folded her arms. "Really?"

I took a deep breath and nodded, my heart hammering in my chest. I was going to have to come clean with her, and that meant spilling the truth about *everything*. It meant opening old wounds which clearly hadn't healed.

God, I don't want to hurt her.

10

CASSIDY

I felt so hurt and frustrated—bordering on angry—that I was digging my nails into the soft flesh of my palms and vibrating. I wanted desperately to let it all out in a torrent of righteous emotion because I was drowning alive inside. But the way Liam kept glancing at me with his gentle eyes and sad frown was blunting my edge. He looked... broken.

Focus, Cassidy.

"Yes, really," he said with a nod. "I was in court all day today. I didn't have the opportunity to get in touch—even though I wanted to, Cass."

Guilt instantly sliced through my belly. Here I was, having a nervous breakdown because he wasn't calling me back when he literally couldn't.

Shame on me.

"Liam, I'm so... sorry," I stuttered. "I didn't know." Silence hung between us, heavy and thick before I found the willpower to continue. "How'd it go? Are you okay?"

"It was only the first day of proceedings, but it got pretty rough in there. It's shit when people try to dig up every shred of dirt, they can on you, and try their darndest to discredit you. My Ex's counsel is set on ruining my reputation."

"I'm so sorry," I whispered, swallowing hard against the feelings that threatened to swallow me up drag me under. I wanted nothing more than to cry! I needed that tangible release. And after such a whirlwind day focused solely on my own feelings, I'd allowed myself to believe all the bullshit my paranoid brain had thrown at me. I felt like a fool.

Maybe that's why they say that we're all fools in love?

"So, that's why I didn't call you back. I had to focus my energy on the case, saying the right things, behaving the right way. It was draining and difficult and honestly... Today was one of the worst days of my life."

My shoulders slumped as I approached him. I had no idea of what to say to him to soothe his stress and pain, but a part of me was sure that words were not what was needed. I placed my hands on his shoulders and pulled him close, allowing him whatever comfort I could give.

It took a few seconds for him to hug me back, but when he did, he lowered his head onto my shoulder and sighed as he held me close.

I could *feel* the pain he was in, and I knew how that felt, to be defeated—bereft. I'd experienced it myself, more than once. When he'd left me, when my mom had died, and when Nathan had his accident and all the bills started to pile up, leaving me feeling lost and helpless.

All the bad things that had ever happened to me began when Liam left. When he hadn't been part of my world, everything went to shit... and it made me wonder.

Is he the key to my life?

Was he the integral part of my world that I was missing and needed to function? Modern society would have us believe that a woman could be happy and successful on her own, and maybe to a degree, there was a grain of truth to that statement. But deep down, no one wants to be alone. We all want to be loved, to have friends and family, or people with whom we can form meaningful connections.

I certainly couldn't speak for everyone, but my heart told me I needed Liam, more than I'd ever dared to admit to myself before. But there was a missing puzzle piece still holding me back from taking the plunge... the uncertainty of why he'd left me so suddenly ten years ago. I still didn't know why things had gone down that way; still didn't know if it was something I did or not. Hopefully, he'd clear it all up... and soon.

Unspeaking, he raked his fingers softly and slowly through my hair.

Waves of desire flowed through me in response, one after the other. And before long goosebumps covered every inch of my body. His muscles relaxed beneath my hands and that's when I realized that this was what I could be for him, and him for me. A safe place, somewhere I could hide away from the world when things got too much to bear. And I could be that for him, too.

We used to be that for each other once upon a time. I would seek refuge at his house when my mother's stupid boyfriend would visit. Luckily, he was only a part of our lives for three years before he left. I sighed against my high school sweetheart. I wasn't trying to kill the mood by dwelling on the past, but after the day I'd had, I was struggling to keep my mind in a positive place. So, I was more than grateful when I felt Liam's hands slip under my shirt, and all the thoughts and negativity fell away.

I glanced up at him and met his gaze. I didn't want to hold back any longer. I couldn't and so I kissed him with all the longing in my soul. There was no more anger inside me or resentment, no more hurt in the moment. Only an uprising of old feelings, and there were *a lot* of them. Tears welled in my eyes and my chest tightened. It wasn't surprising that I'd chosen to bottle my feelings up over the years. They were heart-achingly intense.

Liam kissed me back, his fingers trailing down my spine, before encircling my waist.

I began to tug at his shirt. I needed to feel his skin beneath my hands. I wanted him naked.

He relaxed his arms then and allowed me to take off his t-shirt. He was in great shape.

I loved the look of his chiseled body and reached out to lightly graze my fingers down his chest, all the way to his prominent abs. I sighed in silent contentment. Being able to touch him like this, with so much freedom, after so long was nothing short of blissful.

His strong arms wrapped around me, his stunning green eyes intense and full of yearning.

I tugged off my own shirt, reveling in the warmth of his skin against mine.

He kissed me again, long, and hard, infusing the kiss with everything that had ever been left unsaid between us.

My head spun, leaving me dazed and breathless.

Then he scooped me up in his arms and carried me up the stairs, down a hallway and into his bedroom.

Snuggling close like a damsel of old, I managed a quick look around his sleek, minimalist, adult bedroom, so different from the one he'd had just ten years ago.

He lay me down on his bed as though I was sacred treasure. The mattress was so much softer and more comfortable than the bed we'd shared at the hotel, then he lay down beside me, his heart in his gaze.

And just like that I felt something click inside my chest, like a piece of a long-forgotten puzzle finally finding its place. I was complete. I'd come home.

From there, we undressed each other slowly, like it was our first time again—but everything was different.

Liam kissed my lips softly and tenderly.

My eyes slid shut as his hands explored my body and I allowed mine to explore his. The feeling of his muscles shifting under my touch sent shivers of delight through me. I was already wet for him.

His breathing hitched when he ran his fingers down my thigh. He looked up and met my gaze with his own.

The heat I saw burning there turned me on more than anything else ever could.

He circled my clit with his finger, then added pressure.

I gasped; my whole body was igniting the more he touched me. I could practically already hear the fireworks exploding in my mind. I arched my back, silently willing him to take it one step further. To go deeper. Thankfully, he read my need.

He positioned himself above me, his incredible body suddenly my entire world.

I reached down and ran my fingers lightly down the shaft of his cock and delighted as his entire body tensed in response.

He paused for a moment, letting me stroke him, before he took back control and slid his long, thick cock inside me.

The sensations were amazing and overwhelming. My breath caught in the beauty of the moment. I'd never felt like this before. My heart squeezed with love, with awe... at the raw and pure sensuality of having him against me and inside me.

My lips parted and I sucked in a breath as he filled me up the way only he could.

His rhythm began slow and steady, his thrusts deep, but gentle.

This is the way it's supposed to be with him.

This was no longer merely a physical act anymore. Our union was something more, and I could practically see the emotions flicking through his mind, reflected at me in his clear, green eyes.

Without missing a beat, he began to pick up his pace, quickening his thrusts.

The pleasure inside my belly began to build And I reached up for him, wanting him even closer.

He lowered his torso toward mine, kissing my neck and my chest as he did so. "I've missed this," he breathed against my skin, almost inaudibly.

But I heard him loud and clear.

I have, too.

His breath against my neck made me shiver and I grabbed his shoulders, moaning as the ecstasy grew.

He thrust inside me, pumping faster and deeper, his breathing sexily ragged.

"I've missed this too," I breathed in return.

He raised his face, looking directly at me, our noses touching lightly.

Did I have the courage to say what had to be said? What else did I have to lose at this point? We could only grow from here... "I'm yours, Liam. I always have been."

The corners of his lips curled up before he kissed me, urgently and passionately, his tongue snaking out to taste mine.

Our breathing became quick and ragged, the atmosphere around us thick, heavy, and electric.

My belly was quickening, tightening with my impending release. I glanced up at him, wanting to share everything I could with him. Wrapped my legs around his waist, I grabbed onto his bulging biceps.

Our eyes locked and in that moment, we were the only two people in the world. The only two who mattered. The only two who had *ever* mattered. We pulled one another over the edge, plummeting into oblivion together as our bodies jolted and contracted; sharing one perfect moment of sheer pleasure and pure connection.

My heart sang with happiness as Liam stopped shaking.

He collapsed on top of me, breathing heavily, his skin slick with a fine sheen of sweat.

I brought my hands up and caressed him, running a hand through his hair. This reminded me of our first time, in the back of Liam's dad's truck. We'd been under the stars and wrapped up comfortable blankets which smelled like Liam's cologne. It was beautiful.

Back then we'd talked about our future together, making promises that would never be kept, and vowing we would never let anything tear us apart. That night, I'd hoped those feelings of bliss and happiness would never end. But they did, and so did this one.

Liam rolled off me and lay on his back beside me, wearing a strange expression on his face.

I turned toward him, worry shooting through my heart as my hair tumbled down over my bare shoulders. "Is everything okay?"

Liam glanced at me intently for a few seconds before he moved away and sat upright. Without a word, he slid off the bed and pulled on a pair of comfortable shorts, which he'd retrieved from a nearby dresser. "I can't see you anymore, Cass," he said with a solemn sigh.

I sat bolt upright, holding the blankets to my chest, my heart leaping in my fucking chest. "What?"

He has to be joking.

"I can't see you until everything blows over with the divorce," he replied as he turned to me.

I swallowed hard, my heart pounding in my chest like a bongo drum. I could barely think straight. My world was spinning and falling sideways all at once.

Act, Cassidy. Don't react.

I forced myself to think clearly, to be smart about this. "Is that what your lawyer has advised?" I asked.

He nodded. "Yes, and I think he's right. I can't have anything complicating this case. Especially with you working at my lawyer's firm as well."

Oh. Fuck.

I hadn't realized my new employers would be Liam's lawyers... but it kind of made sense, now that I thought about it. That's how he'd had that connection to begin with. "Um... okay, I get it... I suppose." Well, I was struggling to. "I get that you're both concerned that if people see us together, they'll think we're discussing the case..."

"That's *exactly* the problem. You know that's crucial. Judges forbid it in any case they oversee. Not to mention it brings into question the integrity of my counsel and affords my Ex the opportunity to acquire more ammunition against me. I don't want you getting mixed up with all my mess—any of it."

That sounded a bit... weak. I could refrain from asking or speaking with him about the case. I could be above board. I'd never jeopardize us or my employer's. "But I'm here to support you. You have to know I'd stand by you through this," I said. Then an insidious realization dawned upon me and my gut flared with hurt. "But you don't want me to, do you?" I asked, my heart practically falling out of me.

Liam sighed heavily. "I just don't want to get hurt anymore, Cass."

"Why would I get hurt?" I asked as I slowly stood from the bed, wrapped in the sheet.

Liam put his hands on his hips but didn't say a word.

My jaw dropped as my brain registered the only conclusion I could come up with. He was guilty. "You did it, didn't you?"

"Did what?"

I bit my lip, almost too afraid to say the words out loud. "You actually cheated on her, didn't you?" I'd never thought Liam to be capable of that. Leaving someone, yes. But fucking around on someone who was legally his wife at the time? I'd always thought he was more decent than that, but maybe I didn't know him anymore at all. If that was true, he wasn't the same man I fell in love with all those years ago. He was a different person with a completely different life, and it was being made abundantly clear that there was no room in that life for me.

My heart broke with one all mighty, powerful crack. Tears welled and fell down my cheeks and I swiped angrily at them with the backs of my hands.

Liam was staring at me with wide eyes and eyebrows that had climbed high up his forehead. "You honestly think I would do that? You seriously think I'd cheat on a woman, rather than civilly end the relationship if I was done with them? You should know me better than that, Cass."

I took a few steps toward him, not sure what to believe anymore. If he could cheat on her... what was to stop him cheating on me? My mind filled with dark clouds that rained nothing but doubt and despair.

"I thought I did. I thought I knew you, but the eighteen-year-old version of you, the one I loved, is still that same person who hurt me. The one who left me without even telling me why. Even now, ten years later, you still can't bring yourself to tell me. I loved you with all my heart, and I believed you loved me the same way, but you can't even spare me the decency of telling me what happened! How can I ever trust you or believe you when you won't even explain yourself?" My shoulders shook with emotion as I pleaded my case. "Why did you leave me, Liam?" I had waited over ten years to say that to him, but his expression was more underwhelming than I ever imagined it could be.

He lowered his gaze, which lowered my chances of getting an answer. If I knew anything about this man, it's that he was a runner. He ran away from me, he ran away from the truth, and now he was going to run away from the only chance we might ever have to be together.

I reached down where my clothes lay in a pile. "I'm sick of this, Liam," I said and started to dress. "Don't I deserve to hear the truth?"

"Of course, you do. I just can't tell you."

"You can't me or you won't?" I asked as I pulled my pants up.

Fucking asshole. I can't believe this!

What did it matter now, anyway? Ten years on and he still demonstrated no accountability! He still had no courage to admit that he'd done the wrong thing.

What a coward.

"It's not that simple, Cass," he continued to argue with me.

"Nothing is ever simple with you, though, is it?" I muttered as I slipped my t-shirt over my head.

"I can't, Cass."

"Why not?" I insisted.

He began to turn away, no doubt to avoid explaining himself.

"Liam just tell me! No matter what it is! Just tell me!" I yelled. I was sick to death of all these lies by omission.

He whirled around, his eyes blazing with anger I hadn't expected. "Because your *mom* told me to leave!"

I froze, my vision instantly blurring with impending tears which rushed to the surface faster than I could stop them. "Don't you dare pin this on her!" I fired back. She was dead and couldn't defend herself! Couldn't he just leave her memory in peace?

"It's the truth, Cass. That was why I didn't want to tell you. It's why I couldn't. I didn't want you to hate her after she died," he explained, talking more openly and candidly than he ever had before.

Could it be possible? Would my mom have really sent him away?

My heart lurched anew. "What exactly did she say to you?" I asked quietly, giving him the benefit of the doubt.

"She told me that she wanted you to have everything you deserved in life and that I was going to hold you back. Not literally, of course... but because you loved me so much, she knew you'd have been willing to give everything up for me—to be with the boy from Crest Butte. She wanted you to fulfill all your dreams, not sacrifice them for anyone."

Hot tears stung at the back of my throat and made my eyes water. I could hear those words in her voice echoing in my mind... There was no denying it. She would have done that.

"It wouldn't have been for just 'anyone.' It would have been for you," I corrected, and back then I would have literally done anything for him. I would have given up school, relocated, and had babies the moment he'd wanted them.

Anything for Liam.

He stepped closer, his voice dropping. "You shouldn't do that for anyone, Cass."

"But I would have," I said hopelessly as I recognized the truth in his words. "And I'd do it again if I was given the chance. My life fell apart after you left...and my mom watched me cry myself to sleep for months... and never said anything."

"She just wanted the best for you, like all moms do," Liam offered softly.

I wiped away the tears in frustration, a sob rising in my throat.

What a waste! All that time lost...

All because other people had decided what was best for me.

"So, you think the life I led without you, the emptiness I felt every day, the rejection, and the constant feelings of never being good enough was the best life for me?" I countered as a sad, bitterness arose in me. "Because that's bullshit, Liam."

"You went to UC Denver, just like you wanted. You were first your class!"

I walked away from him and threw my hands up in the air as I fought back the sobs threatening to break me. "Yes, that was *part* of my plan, for sure, but all I ever wanted was you, Liam. Don't you get that? Even now? I understand you wanted me to be happy and have the best possible life, but only I get to decide what that looks like! Not you, or my mom, or anyone else. Me, and only me," I said, wiping away the tears that thickened my throat.

"You don't understand how bad it was for me after you left without telling me why. I had a *constant* ache in my chest. Every sad song I listened to seemed to be about you... the loneliness and heartache; and every happy song reminded me of how *we* used to be, and how close we once were."

"Cass—"

"You know what hurts me the most, Liam? It wasn't because you left—for my benefit, as it turns out—it was the trauma that followed. It was waking up and checking my phone for the messages that weren't there. It was going to sleep, wanting to hear your voice, knowing I'd never hear it again. It was like starting my life over without any idea where to begin. That was how lost I felt. And now you're going to do it again. You're going to leave me high and dry. You aren't willing to risk anything! It's your way or nothing with you."

Liam just stood there like an idiot, falling silent again, reverting to his old, usual ways.

And I couldn't take it anymore. I was pouring my heart out and he was just... standing there. I grabbed my handbag, whirled around, and stomped out of his bedroom, then down the hallway.

"Cass, wait!" he called out after me.

I ran down the steps.

Not this time. Not again. It's too much. It's not love if it's not the same on both sides!

"You have no right to fuck with my feelings. Not again!" I yelled back as I let my emotions wash over me like a tidal wave.

"Cass, please..."

I didn't answer him. I couldn't.

When we reached the bottom of the stairs, he grabbed my hand and spun me around. "I'm sorry, Cass."

"Yeah," I said bitterly as I wiped another deluge of tears from my cheek. "I'm sorry too. I wish I could go back to the day I met you and walk the other way, pretend I didn't see you, because honestly, it would have saved me so much hurt and pain it's fucking ridiculous."

His face fell as hurt rippled through his eyes. "You don't mean that."

"The hell I don't," I snapped, as I broke free of his grasp and left. Tears of anger ran freely as I climbed into my car and drove away, my rage fueling me. I wasn't sure exactly where I was going go, but I put my pedal to the metal and floored it out of there. Maybe the time apart would give me the clarity I so desperately needed.

11

LIAM

It was my turn for my calls to be ignored now, and frankly, I knew I deserved it. I deserved every bit of anger and resentment Cass wanted to throw at me. I'd been wrong to assume I'd known what was best for her. We all had the right to choose our own path in life and only Cass could decide what hers was. Unfortunately, at barely eighteen years old, I hadn't had that presence of mind, I hadn't given her that chance.

Like a lovesick schoolboy I paced around the house, calling her every hour. She'd avoided me entirely since she stormed out of my house last night. And now it was Saturday, so she wasn't at work and unable to answer; she was purposely choosing how she handled our fallout.

She was probably at home, on the couch, covered in her favorite blanket, watching a movie that would only make her cry more. She'd done the same thing when she heard her dad was having an affair with one of the women in our town, and again when one of her best friends walked away from her after a misunderstanding.

I yearned to go over to her house, to try and patch things up, but I also didn't want to make things worse. That was the reason I did what I did back then. I'd loved her too much to stand in the way of her future and her success. I'd wanted her to go to school as she had dreamed of doing, to become an even more amazing woman than she already was. I'd never wanted to make her life worse.

Even now, I still couldn't quite believe how badly I'd screwed everything up again. Even after I'd told her what she wanted to know... I'd still managed to drive her away. I shook my head and collapsed into my recliner. The way she'd stormed out of here last night, tears streaming and heartbroken probably meant she'd never speak to me again. My soul ached at the mere possibility.

No. I have to fix this. I can't leave it like this way.

I'd already wasted a decade without her, I couldn't continue making the same mistakes. I had to tell her everything. I had to admit that even after all these years, I still loved her. I needed to promise that I would never make the mistake of letting her go again and that despite my fuck ups, I hadn't stopped thinking about her since the day I'd left. I had to tell her that I'd been too much of a coward to contact her even in the aftermath.

I just couldn't be that guy anymore. Cass deserved *so* much more. She deserved better, and that was exactly what I was going to give her. I'd give her my *everything*. I was a better man now than the scared boy who'd left the moment Cass's mom had told me to. Regardless of what my shitty divorce case might bring, I had to do this—consequences be damned!

I'll never leave her again.

Grabbing my keys, I jumped in the car, determined to get to Cass as fast as possible. I glanced at the digital clock on the dash and a thought occurred to me. I wasn't going to find her at home, it was after three o'clock. She'd be at the hospital visiting Nathan, her little brother.

I'd kept tabs on Cass and her brother from afar ever since I left home. My dad would phone me regularly, telling me how Cass's mom and Nathan were doing, as well as Cass, whenever she went to visit them, which wasn't very often during her school years. And he'd called me the minute he found out that Cass's mother passed away, and when Cass returned to Crested Butte.

He even spoke to Cass a few times when she'd decided to relocate to Denver after college. I wasn't sure whether he was solely responsible for helping her make the decision to come and start over here, but I sure was grateful.

I drove in the direction of the hospital Nathan was admitted to, and when I noticed Cass's car, I breathed a small sigh of relief. I'd made the right choice. I parked my car a few spots away from hers and hurried to the entrance, not wanting to wait another minute before I saw her again. As I stepped inside, I glanced around, looking for someone to ask for directions. I approached the reception desk.

A middle-aged, red-haired woman smiled warmly at me. "Good afternoon, Sir. Can I help you with something?" she asked.

"I'm looking for Nathan Moore's room."

"Are you a friend or a family member?" she asked.

"A friend. We used to live in the same town. I know his sister, Cassidy," I answered.

"Can I just see some identification, Sir? You're going to have to check in."

"Of course," I said and handed her my driver's license.

She took one look at it, pursing her lips. "You really are from Crested Butte."

"I am."

She handed my license back to me and tapped her finger on the sign-in sheet in front of me. "He's in room two-one-five, second floor."

"Thank you." I quickly filled in the sheet and signed.

She smiled and pointed to her left. "The elevators are that way."

"Thanks." I made my way to the elevator as per the woman's instructions and waited for the elevator doors to open. I stepped inside and pressed the button for the second floor. It only took a couple of seconds until I was hurrying down the hallway towards room two-one-five. I couldn't help the smile that spread across my face as I went, nor the flutter of anticipation that wove through my belly.

When I reached the door, I found it slightly ajar, and I heard voices coming from inside—Cassidy's and Nathan's. I stepped back, pressing my back against the wall and stood quietly. It wasn't my intention to eavesdrop on their conversation, but as soon as I heard my name being mentioned, I could hardly just walk in there.

"Liam's here, in Denver," Cassidy told her brother.

"Liam who broke your heart after high school?" Nathan asked.

"The one and only."

I sighed.

Will I always be that guy?

"What's he doing here? Is he stalking you or something?"

"No, he lives here, actually."

"Have you seen him?" Nathan asked, followed by a long pause. "Oh, no, Cassie. Don't tell me you and Liam—"

"Yes, it happened, okay. Twice."

"Gross. That's way too much information."

"You asked."

I couldn't stop my lips from lifting a little. Cass was nothing if not honest and straight forward; two of the things I loved most about her.

"In all fairness, Cassie, I didn't actually *ask,* but that's beside the point. So, you saw him?"

"Yeah." She sighed. "But nothing about us is easy anymore. We talk, then we end up fighting all the time."

"Well, considering what happened, that's only natural, in my opinion. Plus, it's been what... ten years? You've both probably changed a lot. There's bound to be teething problems."

Out of the mouth of babes

"Some things stay the same, however," Cass added. "Once a scumbag, always a scumbag."

I cringed at Cass's words and rested my head against the wall. Was that really what she thought of me?

"Did you know Mom told him to leave? That she wanted me to achieve everything I wanted without being held back by Liam? By my love... by my feelings for him? She wanted me to have no regrets..."

"And do you? Have no regrets?"

"Oh, I have *a lot* of regrets. And most of them are about *not* being with Liam. When I was with him, I never doubted the way he made me feel or what life held for us. I felt like I was important to him, and I really haven't felt that way since he left."

You were important to me, Cass. You still are.

"Do you still love him?" There was another long pause.

"I never stopped, really, even though he hurt me. He says that he only wanted me to be happy. But I just don't understand it, Nathan. He did that for me, he let me go. Even though I was miserable, and even though I hated him for it... It was such a big sacrifice for him to make. I don't know what to do."

Nathan groaned. "You two make my head spin. You always have."

Cass chuckled. "I think that's the whole dynamic of our relationship. It's not like any other relationship I've ever been in. We're confusing, complicated, and downright impossible sometimes, but our love was real. I just wish... that I could find a way to tell him that."

That's my cue.

I took a deep breath before stepping away from the wall and approached the door. I knocked on it softly and heard Nathan speak again.

"Maybe you still can."

I peered through the opening and both Nathan and Cassidy glanced directly at me.

Cass stood up from the chair beside the bed and stared at me. Her eyes were slightly red, but she looked as beautiful as ever.

"Hey, Liam," Nathan said with a crooked smile. "What a coincidence. We were *just* talking about you."

"You were?" I asked as I entered the room and shook Nathan's hand. "Hey, buddy. Long time, no see. How are you?"

"I'm doing better. I can wiggle my toes now without too much effort. The doctor said that I could go home sooner than planned, which is awesome. Then I get to start physical therapy to learn to walk again. But I'm looking forward to it. I swear I'm never going to sit on my ass ever again after this."

I chuckled and smiled at him. "I'm glad you're doing better, buddy. That accident sounded pretty bad."

"How do you know about the accident?" Nathan asked.

"I have my sources," I shrugged nonchalantly and shot a brief glance at Cass.

She glared at me, her eyes narrowed, and her arms crossed over her chest. "I had to make sure my favorite little slugger was alive and well."

"You're still calling me that?" Nathan muttered and rolled his eyes. "Some things never change, right Cassie?"

Cass cleared her throat and turned to Nathan. "Will you excuse us for a second?"

"Sure, I'll just wait here," Nathan joked. "Good to see you again, Liam."

"Same here, Nathan," I said with a grin.

Cass grabbed my sleeve and practically dragged me out of the room and into the hallway, then she walked down to the next door.

It was an empty private family waiting room, and we both went inside.

She closed the door and rounded on me. "What are you doing here?"

"I came to see Nathan," I answered. "And I knew you'd be here too."

"How did you know I was here?"

"You told me Nathan was in *Sutter Hospital* and I remembered you telling me about the visiting times on Saturdays."

"You remembered all that?" she asked, apparently stunned.

"Cass, I haven't forgotten anything when it comes to you. I remember your fluffy blanket and the way you used to curl up on the couch every time you were sad. I remember how you preferred the left swing on the swing-set because the middle one made you feel unsafe. I remember that you always chewed the tip of your straw before taking the first sip of your soda."

Cass's eyes filled with tears as I spoke, recalling all the things that made me love her more.

The little things. The things that mattered. "And I remember that purple and red mug you used to have. It was the ugliest thing I'd ever seen, but you loved it. You'd take it along to all the football games I forced you to come to, to watch me play."

"I wanted to go," she interjected in a small voice.

"You never told me that," I said, my brow furrowing. "I thought you hated football."

"I do," she admitted. "But I went because *you* were playing."

"You've always made sacrifices for me, Cass, and I didn't want to be the reason you didn't get to go to college. Who the hell was I to stand in your way?"

"You were the love of my life, and before last week, *you* were the one who got away! The one I would always think of whether I was with someone else or not. The one I would always compare everyone else to. There was no one who ever came close to you, Liam."

I took a step toward her. "I wanted you to have an amazing life, Cass."

"I *had* an amazing life with you in it, Liam. Why couldn't you see that?"

I could and I'd loved our lives together, but her mom had been so convincing in her argument that I'd hold her back from her full potential... "You weren't the only one who felt undeserving, you know?" I sighed.

"What are you talking about?"

"I never thought I was good enough for you, Cass. And when your mom came to talk to me and said it would be better if I left and allowed you the freedom to be something better—it just made sense. Your mother never liked me anyway if I'm honest. She told me that I was making a rebel out of you."

She smiled softly, the ghost of a memory behind her eyes. "That's probably because you reminded her of my dad when he was young. He was charming and spontaneous too. She was probably afraid that you would hurt me the same way my dad hurt her."

"I'm not your dad," I said defensively. "I would never cheat on you, Cass. Never. I'd never do it to anyone. I haven't, you have to believe me."

"I know," she acknowledged. "At least you have the courage to admit to your mistakes."

"It's taken me a while, but I do," I answered and approached her. Her hand was inches away from mine and I reached out to take it.

Instead, she took mine, beating me to the punch line. "Say what you want to say, Liam. Right now."

I took a deep breath and looked her directly in the eyes. "I'm not going to stand here and tell you all the things I've done wrong in my life because we'd be here all goddamn day, but I *will* say that I'm sorry, *truly* sorry for the pain I've caused you. You deserved better, but at the time, I thought I was protecting you from me, when in fact I was depriving you of the one thing you always taught me. To love and be accepted."

Cass smiled, her eyes filling with tears again, but she pursed her lips to prevent them from spilling down her cheeks.

"My life is complicated, messy, and stressful right now, but there is one thing I am sure of, and that is that I love you, Cassidy Moore. And that will never, ever change."

Cass cocked her head. "I've waited *so* long to hear you say that, and it was worth every single minute of waiting." she whispered,

I pulled her close and our lips met in a moment that was overdue by a decade. It was a moment filled with so much love and understanding that it overwhelmed me and threatened to bring me to my knees. I felt humbled and grateful in the very same breath.

Our lips parted slowly, and Cass glanced up at me, her eyes shining with happiness as she shed her tears without shame. "Why did you have to make me fall so hard for you?"

"I'm so sorry, sweetheart," I murmured.

"I bet you are," she countered as she smiled before pulling a little further away. "About what I said to you, Liam... I didn't mean most of it. I know you're not the kind of guy to cheat on a woman. You've always been respectful and caring. I'm sorry I insulted you like that. And I know you'd never lie to me about something so serious, either. I'm sure it feels like your integrity is on the line and this divorce is going to get harder before it gets any better—we both know that—but I am *here* for you if you'll let me be."

I squeezed her hands. "I don't want to pull you into my complicated life."

She laughed. "Our life has been complicated since the day we met, so I'm kind of used to it." She wrapped her arms around my shoulders. "We'll get through this together, okay? I promise. All you have to do is let me in."

I glanced down at her, my heart swelling. "Thank you. And I'm sorry I pushed you away when I needed you the most, and when you needed me, too."

"We all make mistakes, Liam. It's how we handle the repercussions of those mistakes that matter."

My mouth curved into a smile, and I brushed a lock of blonde hair from her face. "For years, when people asked me if I had any regrets about my past, I used to just say your name, and that you were the one who got away."

"Well, you never have to say that ever again. I'm yours forever, I always have been, and I always will be," she smiled at me, her magnificent blue eyes glittering with sincerity.

At that moment, in the private family waiting room of the hospital, with her arms wrapped around my shoulders, and her eyes sparkling just like the first day I'd met her, I was home. I was done running. And it was right then I realized that home wasn't a place—it never was. It was where my heart felt the safest. And mine was with hers. No matter what the future held for us, I'd dedicate the rest of my life to seeing her smile and making up for the time we'd lost.

"I love you, Cass," I whispered, my heart in my throat as I brought my lips to hers once more. "Always and forever."

The End.